DEAD FUNNY

ROBIN INCE is a multi-award-winning comedian and author. His book *Robin Ince's Bad Book Club* was based on his tour *Bad Book Club*. More recently he has toured *Happiness Through Science*, *The Importance of Being Interested* and is currently touring *Robin Ince Is In And Out Of His Mind* and *Blooming Buzzing Confusion*.

JOHNNY MAINS is an award-winning editor, author and horror historian. He is editor of Salt's *Best British Horror* series and five other anthologies, and author of two short story collections.

DEAD FUNNY

HORROR STORIES BY COMEDIANS

Edited by
ROBIN INCE
and
JOHNNY MAINS

SALT

CROMER

PUBLISHED BY SALT
12 Norwich Road, Cromer, Norfolk NR27 0AX United Kingdom

'Possum' previously published in *The New Uncanny* (Comma
Press, 2008) ed. Sarah Eyre and Ra Page

'A View From A Hill' previously published in *New Statesman*
(December, 2012)

Printed in Great Britain by Clays Ltd, St Ives plc

Typeset in Sabon 9.5/12

ISBN 978 1 907773 76 1 hardback

1 3 5 7 9 8 6 4 2

Dead Funny is dedicated to
Rik Mayall and Robin Williams

Robin Ince would also like to dedicate *Dead Funny*
to Nicki and Archie

Johnny Mains would also like to dedicate *Dead
Funny* to Kevin Demant from the *Vault of Evil*
website and Bob Pugh

CONTENTS

INTRODUCTION

I WAS LUCKY enough to find a sheep's skull in a field when I was ten, and soon it was on my bedside table, with a candle stuck on it to replicate some imagined cover of a horror anthology. I was that child who hung around cemeteries, collected LPs of death and horror sound effects and Edgar Allan Poe readings by Basil Rathbone, and was told by his older sisters that, if and when he grew up, he'd become a serial killer. I became a stand-up comedian instead. On the advice of the Pope of Trash, John Waters, I have committed my hideous crimes as comedy routines rather than in actuality.

It all started with Alan Frank's Horror Movies book. I still have it now, though stupid nine year old me cut out some of the colour plates to make into a wastepaper bin as a project at the Friday night Baptist church children's group. It would be some time before I would see my first proper horror. At ten, I saw Vincent Price in *The Pit and the Pendulum*. At eleven, I was allowed to watch the black and white half of the BBC horror double bill season. I wrote to Boris Karloff's widow and she sent me a lovely letter back.

All things horror were embraced by the outsider kids of my generation. We spent our pocket money on *House of Hammer* magazine and trading cards with a stick of yellow gum and images of Christopher Lee's Dracula impaled on a cartwheel. I bought the *Mayflower Book of Black Magic Stories* and picked up Herbert Van Thal's *Pan Book of Horror Stories*. The first I remember reading was by Dulcie Gray, an actor who specialised in playing well-bred couples with her husband Michael Denison, but I discovered that behind this prim and proper exterior was a mind that reveled in the grotesque. The outlet for being trapped in stagey, sometimes stodgy fare, was to kill and kill again on the page.

The comedians and writers I usually hang out with were usually the slightly weird kids at school, while others collected football stickers, they hung around comic shops trying to get hold of *Monster Mag* and imagining whole films in their heads from single stills of decapitated Shakespearians or frozen Nazis. We had nightmares, but rather than destroying us, we fed on them, and one day they'd become our day job. I still read Poe now, and I even got around to a one off, late night improvised prog rock musical with Robyn Hitchcock and a bunch of jazz musicians, mimes and opera singers, based on Guy N Smith's killer crabs novels.

And while you are reading this book, remember that the goriest deaths will have been created while the writer was imagining their worst heckler. Interrupt at a comedy club at your peril, now you know what goes on in the minds of the stand-up.

As to the traumatic birth of this book, I 'met' editor Johnny Mains in 2010 through Twitter. I was due to play in Norwich, where he was then living. He asked if we could chat about the *Pan Horrors* after my show, which we did.

Over several beers, Johnny made less sense as the evening went on and he forgot his coat.

We met again when I came to Plymouth in 2011 with 'Night of 400 Billion Stars'. He came to me with the idea of co-editing Dead Funny and it was something I immediately said yes to. However, Johnny and I are both hectically busy people and we never got round to working on the book until this year. But here it is. A book that we're both extremely proud of, we've not had to kill any comedians during the making of it and I'd like to thank Johnny for all of his hard work.

ROBIN INCE

FOREWORD

I ALWAYS THINK that a good story becomes a truly great one that it has a smattering of black humour to it. The stories of Conrad Hill and Harry E. Turner, both authors of the infamous *Pan Book of Horror Stories* series were able to, quite magically, mix disgusting horror and stomach ache laughter very easily.

It was during a chat about what anthology to do next with my wife when we hit upon the idea that an anthology by comedians would be a suitably quirky book. It's certainly never been done before. The more I thought on the concept, the more I was excited by it; comedians write their own material and it can stray into very dark places at times. Why couldn't they write short stories?

I had known Robin Ince for about a year by this time. I had commissioned a short story from both he and Charlie Higson, and what I was sent for *The Screaming Book of Horror* only confirmed the fact that a horror anthology, written by comedians, just *might* work.

So I asked Robin if he would co-edit the book with me. Robin said yes, then the work of finding a publisher began. Although interested, several publishers said no. They were impressed by the names we could bring to the book, but all said that horror anthologies didn't sell any more. One publisher even laughed down the phone at me.

Finally, I found a publisher that was really excited by the idea, Salt. It's another example of Indie publishers venturing into territory where the mainstream fear to tread.

And bless them, they've been brilliant to work with.

So here is *Dead Funny*. Horror stories by comedians. It's an experiment in terror. Not all of the stories will make you laugh. Some of them might make you vomit or be scared to go outdoors after 6 p.m.

I'm so very proud of this book. It's been a surreal experience to work on but a delight to do. Thank you to Robin Ince who is a very canny co-editor and also the authors who have written some excellent stories. I really do hope you enjoy them as much as I have.

JOHNNY MAINS

DEAD FUNNY

REECE SHEARSMITH

DOG

I HAVE NEVER liked dogs. I find them dirty and stupid and totally worthless. I don't understand the mind of anyone that has a dog. How can you possibly find time to care for it? Let it stink out your home? Walk alongside it, scooping up its hot shit off the pavement and grass? 'Let's go for a lovely walk . . . oh, don't forget the little plastic bag to scoop up the endless shit that this creature is going to squeeze out along the way.' Never mind about the piss. It can piss anywhere it likes. I know that you are thinking that I sound unreasonable. People are very protective of these idiot creatures. I find it bizarre. They are of no value. I have no time for dog owners and their beasts.

I suppose, as an introduction that might be called 'setting out my stall', I must at this point explain my position. I am not too deluded to recognise that my views at first may sound extreme; but I must insist that you hear me out. As you will see – it all comes to bear.

From the age of about 11, summer holidays were spent with my grandparents. I would be taken on day trips to the seaside and the stately homes of the North of England. It was a curiously pious way to spend the long stretch between the summer and autumn terms of school. I found nothing odd about it, apart from, of course, the pervading sadness that sullied most of the enforced merriment. Sadness because in the time before I was fostered off to my grandparents I'd had my own two functioning parents and a super little brother who I loved very much. My brother's name was Elliot. I knew him for ten years before he was killed and both my parents went mad with the grief of it. You're probably thinking you have cottoned on to the gist of my tragic tale, and have leapt to the conclusion that my brother was killed by a dog. A dog attack. Mauled and bitten. But that is not what happened. Little Elliot was killed by a dog, yes – but it was ultimately far worse than had he simply been savaged by one. Elliot died of toxocariasis, the disease that hides in dog shit, blinding those that fall foul to it. Thus my brother went blind first. And being blind after having had sight is a hell that I would not wish upon anyone. Except dog owners. For it was dog owners on a day out without, I presume, a little plastic bag about them, that sealed my brother's fate. Elliot was blinded by the disease that lives in dog faeces, and two years after he lost his sight, he was struck down and killed, having wandered sightlessly into the path of a van delivering cakes. The detail of the cake van is slightly absurd I know, but to mention Mr Kipling only seems to make it worse.

I heard the accident first. I was in the garden with my parents. Then a screech and a thud. The sound of my brother's death. I remember hoping selfishly, as time seemed to slow down and swim around me, that it wasn't Elliot. Not for his sake, but for mine. I would be in such trouble if he had been hurt when he was now so much my responsibility. I had been his eyes since the dog shit took his away. It's odd, but up until his actual death, the guilt had always been 'Who let him touch the dog shit?', 'How did he end up with it in his eyes?' After this – his actual death – there could be no ambiguity about who was to blame. It was me. Ironically enough all because I took my eyes off him. When we ran outside the driver was already out of the van and trying to pull Elliot out from under the front wheels. I remember how upsetting it was to see the man tugging on his limp arms. Even then I thought it was probably wrong to be pulling on him like that, but I think the man was in shock. He was shouting that he hadn't seen him and 'There was no time to stop', and even more curiously, 'I'm not from round here'. The rest is as horrible as you might expect. Rushing and screaming and crying and misery. I hope you didn't think this was going to be anything but nasty. There is no way of wrapping these events up nicely.

So as you can see, my childhood was ruined by a dog. It can be traced back. It is, unfortunately, that simple. The story – if I am actually even telling one (I'm not so sure that I am) – doesn't end there. My brother and his death was one thing. But my revenge – my revenge on the lady that owned the dog, the original dog that blinded my brother – that is another thing.

It must read as unusual, I suppose, to wait so long over such a matter. I can imagine hastier people, once they had a lightning rod singled out for their rage and injustice, just kind of getting on with it. But not me. I waited. Initially I had to, as it wasn't clear, as I have already stated, 'Who let him touch the dog shit'. It was in months of nights alone with my brother, sat in the dark with him, to be at one with him, that I coaxed out of him the exact moment that he came into contact with the disease toxocariasis. We were able to whittle it down – over many months of talking – to an incident in our local park. Strangely enough, now without his sight, Elliot became almost bat-like with his hearing, and his sense of smell was also heightened. Doesn't really do it for me, as far as a trade of the senses. All you really need to be able to do is see. Take smell away if you must. But in this instance, the curious amplification of Elliot's other senses helped us triangulate and hone in on the day he fell in the excrement. The smell overwhelmed him to recall it. I could almost smell it myself. But alongside this was the voice of the owner – a woman, with a shrill high-pitched rather condescending tone – that Elliot was able to recall and ultimately, crucially, recognise again. Elliot remembered the woman berating him more than the dog. 'Shuffling around in it like that – you've made an awful mess!' As though Elliot himself were responsible for shitting in the park.

It is an awful feeling when, having done nothing wrong, you start to feel like you are being painted as the 'baddie'. I began to feel like that after we killed the first dog. Yes, I know I didn't mention it earlier, but it took time to find the right woman and dog responsible. We did in fact get through several others before we uncovered Mrs Lovelever. It was quite fortunate in a way, as quite by accident (and I suppose you could call them 'accidents') we were able to hone what we were doing, until we were quite skillful at it. Bear in mind, it was all me really, as Elliot was of little help. He could hardly be used as a 'look out'. Basically we would sit in the park or I would orchestrate walking alongside dog walkers (after our talks I had narrowed it down to older ladies) and invariably because of his white stick they would always strike up conversation with us. It is insult to injury that the blind are so instantly pitiable. I knew people that would cry just at the sight of Elliot. A small boy, smelling his way through the world, when he should be out climbing trees, playing football or cycling down country lanes. It was a combination of all that AND the tragic wearing of the blacked-out spectacles that left him looking so sad. I always found them so final. The curtain is down. Nothing to see here. No point in pretending that any light will ever get through. All boarded up. After getting the ladies chatting I would ask them about their dog as a way of getting them to talk at length (and they always would) so that Elliot with his bat-like hearing could have a good listen and decide if we were, in fact, in the company of our target. It would never take very long for Elliot to dismiss ones that were definite 'no's'. It was harder when he wasn't sure. The signal for a 'no' was Elliot would give a cough. If he wasn't sure he would remain silent. It used to frighten me when he stayed quiet. My heart would race in the minutes that passed, as it would become more and more possible that we had finally found the person responsible. Sometimes the women would ask Elliot if he wanted to stroke their dog. It was always a queasy moment. We decided that it was always best to say yes. It made the women feel good, like they were giving Elliot purpose for a few seconds. 'His miserable life isn't all that miserable today, he touched my dog for thirty seconds and it licked him.' Pathetic.

The first time it happened, that Elliot thought we had the right woman, I nearly passed out in fear. My heart was pounding anyway because he hadn't dismissed her with a cough. I think he was unnerved too and he let her say her goodbyes and leave before gasping, 'I think that's her.' I needed it confirmed immediately.

'Are you sure?'

'I think so. Yes.'

When it came to the next step, it felt very much like passing through a door into something you knew would change your life forever. People in normal life don't do what we were doing. Spending, in fact, a LOT of time doing. It was obsessional, but it felt in check because I recognised it was obsessional. When a woman was a distance away, we would wait for her to be separated from her dog, this was before they had those long ball throwers with what looks like an ice cream scoop at the end, so we relied on sticks or balls thrown by hand that would send the dogs running off into the woodland that surrounded the park. Of course it didn't always happen so smoothly. Some never let their dog off the lead, so they were reluctantly abandoned. But it was quite an easy task to get the dog once it was in the woods and simply take it home with us via a footpath through the trees. The owners would be left calling for their mutt from the edge of the green, not realising at that point they were never going to see it again.

Now then. Killing a dog. You won't want to hear this. We did it in the shed, and not always when my parents were out. I don't know why. It did occur to us that there might be noise and barking etc., but I think we felt untouchable. I could always imagine a scenario of being caught, but equally imagine being able to explain it all away. The first one we killed was hard because it was the first one. In actual fact, it should have been easy as it was a very little dog; one of those that look more like a rat. It never ceases to amaze me that people spend any time on these creatures, putting red bows on their heads and stuff. Anyway. Elliot stood in the corner panting; the dog was running round in circles. I think it was excited because it was in a new place. It took some courage to even decide how I was going to kill it, and it was made worse by having to narrate everything every step of the way for Elliot's benefit. It made it all very firm and real. I think it might have stayed more in my head, not having to say it all out loud, if you know what I mean. I pulled down a hammer, hanging from two nails on the shelf, and braced myself.

'What have you got? What have you got?' hissed Elliot. The first strike: I missed it and hit the floor. The dog barked and growled at my act of aggression. After that point it occurred to me I might end up bitten, so I quickly thought of something. I grabbed a hessian garden waste bag that was crumpled up in the corner and threw it over the dog. It got out from under it quickly enough, and it took several goes to get it covered and then stand on the bag either side of the dog, pinning it tight to the ground underneath. But I did it. It was then much easier to hit the bulge in the middle of my legs without feeling nearly half so sickened. It squeaked on the first hit, then kind of whistled, then stopped altogether after about twenty smacks with the hammer. I don't know why but I started counting the blows out loud, like it was an important part of the process. As if there was a correct number I had to get to. I suppose I stopped at twenty because it was a round number. Elliot said, 'Is it dead? What does it look like?' and it was in his asking what it looked like that all remorse or sadness or upset for what I had just done, completely and utterly disappeared. Fuck this stupid cunt dog. My brother was blind because of it. It deserved to die. I lifted up the sack. At first I couldn't pull it away from the mess underneath. I had hit so hard in places that the material was pushed in and out of the dog and it was mangled. I stopped bothering in the end and folded the whole thing in on itself and took it to a bin in the park. I just walked along casually, with Elliot of course, and put the whole lot in the rubbish like it was nothing.

The realisation that there were flaws in our plan came very quickly. On our way home from the park, after the first killing, we passed a woman talking to a sandy-coloured Labrador and Elliot whispered to me, 'Oh God, I think that's her.' And thus it began. A spate of dog killings. Each one satisfying in the moment,, but lasting only as long as it took to walk past another possible candidate. Curiously, I never got annoyed about it. Elliot was blind, how was he supposed to know? Ultimately we realised this was going to be a little bit trial and error. Once that was understood, it was actually – and I don't mean for this to sound ghoulish – quite fun. Aside from the fact they were all mistakes in regard to them being the wrong dogs, in our eyes (ha) they weren't – because they were still dogs. We had moved beyond our own feeble search for justice, and our punishment had become far more encompassing. This was about the eradication of a much bigger problem. And so it followed that we began experimenting with different ways to kill dogs. I remember one spate of killings that were purely about how quickly and succinctly it could be done. Finding that 'sweet spot' that, with one blow, would kill it instantly. (I had read they kill pigs this way) I never managed it with one, but I think I did do it in three once. Anyway. We once tried to drown one, but it didn't work, it kept getting out and splashed and thrashed most of the water away. And a paddling pool is not the best receptacle to drown an angry dog in fighting for its life. We needed a tin bath really.

Other methods included cutting all the legs off first, then finally the head. This could only be attempted with the more ratty dogs as I previously stated. We tried injecting one using an old icing sugar pipe. Didn't really work. Annoyed, I think we blow torched it with an old aerosol can. Stank the shed out though.

I can't remember when we decided that we had been getting it all wrong and it was the owners of the dogs who were actually to blame and not the dogs themselves. (The irony of this part is that some of you will be less appalled at our killing of the old women than the killing of their stupid fucking dogs.) I do know when it was, actually: we were sat watching *That's Life* with Mum and Dad. Cyril had just done a funny limerick, and there was one of the many awkward segues into something more serious from Esther, when she turned her attention (yet again) to some child abuse or other, as was often the way. It was always shocking, but made worse because only moments before we had seen one of the team burst into song at a garden centre and grab a passer-by and made her join in. What I got from this report, which was about cruelty to animals, was that people who owned the animals seemed to be getting the blame. What I didn't get from the report was any pang of guilt that I had been cruel to animals. It never even occurred to me. It just made me shift focus from the animals to the people.

The first old woman (Elliot assured me she was the one) was very sweet really, and accompanied us back to our house without any fuss. I told her that poor, blind Elliot wasn't feeling very well and would she mind seeing that we got home alright. As I have said, people go a little bit weird around blind people – silly really since they are the one set of people that can't see how you are (or are not) behaving, but she readily said of course she would help. Her dog was big. I was secretly pleased we were going to kill her and not it. I wouldn't have known where to begin, but as we walked along I thought, she would easily fit into two rubbish bags. We got to our house and I told her, if she wouldn't mind, to put her dog in the shed, just out of the way, as our mum was allergic. She said of course and once she was in there I grabbed the dog hammer (did I mention it became known as the dog hammer?) and smacked her on the head with it. She was puzzled at first and sort of bent double. This gave me a nice pop at the back of her head which I hit with the claw part and wrenched free, pulling off part of her scalp and a bit of skull, I thought. Anyway, she was easy and it all went well. The annoying part was the 'get rid', which took ages as despite being little, she was still bigger than what I'd been used to. I don't remember how many more we killed. I think probably about eleven or twelve. They all merge into one when I think back. There's the odd funny detail: one of them, I remember, her false teeth flew out when I hit her head. I was laughing and Elliot was saying, 'What? What's funny about it?' It was ages before I could tell him, I was laughing so much. Another one tried, quite quickly after the first blow, to grab me; she was quite strong. I hit her again and then, as she burbled on the floor, I cut her feet off with a saw. I chopped them off with her shoes still on, but I concede it was done in spite because she had actually managed to scratch me. (I told my mum that I must have done it playing. She didn't care.) I don't know why I did this, but because a lot of them were old, they nearly all wore glasses and so I began keeping them. I had about eight pairs when we finally met Mrs Lovelever.

I knew it was going to be different when, as usual, we sidled up to her and I got her talking. Her dog was a collie, which I hated. When she spoke the dog ran off and she shouted in a clipped Barbara Woodhouse voice for it to come back. Elliot went white. I saw the colour drain from his face. I felt sick. He didn't need to say or do any more. I knew this really was her. And that dog – that actual Lassie lookalike dog – was the cause of Elliot being blind. We both stood there for a moment and then I managed to get things back on track. I quickly used Elliot looking awful to ask if she would mind taking us home. At first, because I presumed she was a horrible cow, I worried she might not agree to it, but once again the blind card worked and she came back with us.

It was a long walk home. I wanted to have time to talk to Elliot. I wanted to ask him how he wanted me to do it. Did he have a preference? What had he particularly enjoyed the sound of? As it was, we got home and I did the usual thing of getting her to go to the shed. Elliot stood in the garden, almost too afraid to come in. His new role – since we had just been killing the owners – was to take hold of the dogs on their leads; get them out of the way whilst I did the deed. But he just stood there.

'Come on, Mandy. Inside!'

The old woman barked her order but the dog ran off. Elliot stumbled after it, out of the garden. I told Mrs Lovelever he would bring Mandy back. It occurred to me, once we were standing in the shed, that Mrs Lovelever hadn't recognised the new blind version of Elliot. I couldn't help myself.

'You don't remember my brother, do you?' I said.

'Who?' she said.

'My brother. Elliot. The blind boy we walked home with.'

She looked confused and it made me feel incredibly angry. She didn't even have the decency to remember the incident.

'He got your dog's shit on him and he went blind because of it.'

It was then that she started trying to leave the shed. I was annoyed that Elliot wasn't there to see it, but of course he wouldn't see it. I grabbed a screwdriver and stabbed her with it. She tumbled back and held the stab wound. After that she couldn't speak. She tried to but all that came out was a kind of low gurgling. It was odd out of an old woman's mouth. I finished her off quite quickly. It was not at all as I had imagined, but it is different when you go through the door. I had learnt that. It's never as you imagine. I think there had simply been too much build up. It was like Christmas or birthdays. It was just over and done and that was that. I killed the dog as well of course. THE dog. I strangled it with wire. When I emerged from that stinking shed, dragging the dead dog on a wire behind me, my mother and father were standing there. There was no sign of Elliot.

They looked at me in disbelief, appalled, I presumed, at the sight of the dead dog. I thought: wait until you see inside the shed!

'Where's Elliot?' I said. That was when we heard it. Screech and thud. The sound of my brother's death. He had run out into the road chasing the very dog that had blinded him in the first place, and was knocked down dead by a Mr Kipling van. Big cherry bakewells pictured on the side.

Both Mrs Lovelever and her dog Mandy survived. I suppose because an ambulance was called they managed to save her. My brother – not so lucky. I went into a home as I was considered 'troubled'. I never needed to admit to the other murders of either the dogs or the owners. I just said we wanted revenge and had targeted Mrs Lovelever. It was a 'one off'. My grandparents looked after me when my parents couldn't bear to look at me anymore. Which I thought fair enough. The day trips they said were to 'normalise' me.

It was a long time ago now. I still don't like dogs. It was only recently they told me I never had a brother called Elliot. But that can't be right. I still have his stick and glasses.

SARA PASCOE

A SPIDER REMEMBER

I THINK WE loved each other. It's difficult to remember what he was like before. At least I know what's happening to me, which makes it less scary.

Or much worse.

I *said* I loved him, out loud, to his face. And to other people. I like to get intense with my partners, analytical late nights drinking and listening to great music. I have a record player, which puts some people off me. Especially the neighbours. I felt very close to him for that first year. I was thinking about getting a tattoo of his name; I'd never done that for a boyfriend before, except once.

He was very tall, so people always commented and made the same jokes and he had to repeat the same passive aggressive responses. I got neck pains when we kissed standing up. An achy echo of him remaining for hours after a lovely date. He was laid down at the end, so it would have been easier to kiss him. But I didn't. He was no longer him.

Even after a year, we were still learning about each other's minds and behaviours. Despite the jazz-underscored introspective conversations at my flat, I didn't even know he was scared of spiders until he woke up that night: 'It's on my face, it's ON MY FACE!'

I'm sitting here now wondering why the government are covering this up. If I'd had any idea of the danger . . . but then I guess no one would ever go to sleep at all. Die from that instead. That's what happens: seven days without and then you're gone. And psychosis from the third day, so there *are* similarities.

'You're dreaming,' I had told him. And not politely. I hated him for waking me up.

He was moving around stupidly. 'I can feel it, it's on my face.'

'It's just a bloody dream.'

'IT'S A SPIDER.'

He swam his lengthy limbs and I went back to sleep.

In the morning he showed me it. Dead. He'd held it in his hand all night to prove that I should have been more sympathetic. Which pissed me off.

'It's still just an insect.'

He was being so childish. 'It was running over my face.'

'You're lucky you don't live in Africa or something, or the jungle.'

'I choose not to live there, because I hate spiders.'

'You can't choose where you're born.'

'I would have moved.'

It wasn't an enjoyable row. There was no relief afterwards from having purged a poison, found new equanimity. It was petty and I wasn't going to apologise for not helping him kill an arachnid in the night. He needed to grow up about it. He sulked for the afternoon; I wished he'd leave. We watched TV to avoid talking. I made an excuse about an early morning to ensure I went to bed alone. When we caught each other's eye we pretended to smile.

Dinner that weekend was planned. I had a feeling he was planning to break up with me, the arrangements seemed so formal, and we hadn't 'made up' properly. Our phone calls had been lists of what we had done, no laughter. I should have apologised, I look back now and wish I'd been nicer, but I didn't know.

In the restaurant I thought he seemed thinner in his face and a bit pale. Fragile. This is definitely it, I thought, despising him in preparation. We ate in virtual silence, my contempt for him oppressed me. He slumped with his head in his hands when offered a dessert menu.

He was so rude to the waiter. 'No. I can't. Can you go away? I have to tell her something.'

The poor guy left. Another poor guy looked at me.

'Kate . . .'

I made my face ready to say, 'That's fine, babe. That's what I want too, to just be friends or . . .'

'I can still see him.'

'Who?' I looked around for the waiter.

'The spider I killed.'

'What spider that you killed?'

'The one who lived in your house.'

I was relieved. Stupidly laughing. I must have loved him, I could breathe again, hysterically happy. His face folded into itself as he cried.

'I'm sorry, babe, I thought you were going to break up with me.' I spoke softly and tried to reach him across the table. 'I'm not making fun of you.'

'It runs about my eyes.'

It was difficult to hear him, he was telling himself more than me.

'I can see it, around the edges, and then straight across my . . .'

I watched him cry and realised he was mad.

I took him home with me that night, feeling responsible and not wanting to be. I lied positively, about a doctor helping him. I was thinking anti-hallucinatory drugs, he imagined some arachnid-killing eyewash. He left in the night and I didn't wake up. I hoped he would be okay but didn't know what I could do.

I could've phoned him or believed him but I didn't.

Four days later he found his way back somehow. Maybe a taxi had dropped him because he didn't seem sure where he was. Banging on the door woke me up, the last restful night I'll ever have. He dribbled words, dropping them separately and widely apart. A doctor. No one believed. Worse now. Many many. So lots. Prison. The hospital.

'Do you want me to take you?'

I needed to call someone, I couldn't deal with this on my own.

He shook his head and walked in circles around the room. Less and less control of his limbs as I watched him. His words became noises. I rang for an ambulance, gave them all the details. 'It's a psychotic attack, he thinks he has spiders in his eyes.'

His hands swiped at his eyes as he swirled about the room. I was reminded of zombies. A body living with no one left living in it. The doorbell squawked as he fell flat on his face. I heard his nose break, and I saw the back of his head.

His hair was moving.

Screaming, I ran to the door, tried to get out as the paramedics pushed their way in. They were wrapped in plastic, now I know why. There was a woman in a suit, she caught my arm, held me back.

'They're in his hair, they're in his hair,' I tried to explain to her.

She shushed me angrily and pulled me into the front room, we stood near my record player. Next to the sofa. Where I used to chat and drink and live.

They were wrapping him in clear plastic sheeting and I could still see the red rim under his hair. The edge of the nest, as they streamed out, hundreds of spiders swarming from his skull. Small, tiny, harmless spiders.

'It doesn't usually get as far advanced as this. It's a bad case. I'm sorry about your friend,' the woman said, not sounding sorry.

'It's disgusting,' I said. I should have been sick or something, done something human. Instead I just stood there as she gave instructions to the crew. Tests. Incineration. Lies about cause of death to relatives.

Outside there was an ambulance and a smaller unmarked van. I got in the back without asking any questions. I couldn't talk, everything was shut off. I thought about calling a lawyer, or someone from work. I thought I saw a spider.

Only natural, after all that had just happened. Of course I itched a bit. My skin prickled and crawled, I kept imagining I could feel tiny legs running over my body. They had lived in the mind of someone I loved.

We drove for hours. My feet and legs fell asleep and I couldn't feel them. And after a couple of peripheral jolts, I saw it properly. It ran straight across. Across the world, all I could see of it. The biggest thing and the nearest thing and it was already inside me.

And now I try not to panic. I sit in a contained cell asking them to kill me. But they won't, they don't understand enough yet, they need to study how it happens. The effects. They aren't even kind, because I'm revolting to them. And so the spiders dance, more of them every hour, I watch them and they are all the world. And every person who knows what I am going through is dead already. And I know how he felt. And it's too late to console him.

I wish I believed in heaven.

MITCH BENN

THE PATIENT

DAY 1,271

IT WAS RAINING as Dr. Barber walked up the drive to his front door.

Even now, after all this time, entering the house caused him a twinge of pain. Once, long ago, his arrival would have been greeted with noise and happiness. Now there was silence. Bleak, numb silence.

The house was comfortable enough; there were plush upholstered chairs and sofas, a well-appointed kitchen (a little less state of the art now than when it had been installed), a large though seldom watched TV . . . but no photographs. No photographs anywhere. They'd been removed. Re-purposed.

Dr. Barber put the kettle on and surveyed the meagre contents of his fridge. Perhaps he'd phone for Chinese later. Perhaps he wouldn't bother. He wasn't always hungry afterwards. Although curiously, on occasion, he was ravenous.

Dr. Barber stirred his tea and got up. In his haste to begin the session, he almost forgot to take with him the little paper bag he'd brought back from the hospital. He snatched it from the kitchen counter and went out into the hall.

The floor of the hall was carpeted; kneeling down at the living room doorway, Dr. Barber found the split in the carpet with his fingertips and rolled a section back, revealing polished wooden floorboards and a hinged trapdoor.

Dr. Barber hooked his finger into the trapdoor's brass ring catch release, twisted it, felt the click and, grunting with effort, lifted the hatch open. He reflected that a day would surely come when he lacked the strength to do this, but the experiment would probably be over by then.

The hatch required effort to lift because it was thick and heavy; a three-quarter inch section of pine floorboard lay on top of two inches of polyurethane sound-proofing foam. This foam layer extended under the whole floor. Dr. Barber had had it installed before the experiment began. He'd told the insulation company that his daughter wanted to convert the cellar into a recording studio.

There was no studio.

There was no daughter.

Through the open hatch Dr. Barber could see the ladder extending down into the cellar. The lights were on in the cellar. The lights were always on.

Dr. Barber descended the ladder with a little difficulty: one hand held both his tea and the bag from the hospital. He struggled down the ladder one-handed, put the tea and the bag down on one of the shelves lining the cellar walls, then ascended a couple of steps, reached up and pulled the heavy hatch closed with its familiar solid-sounding clunk.

Dr. Barber took a sip of tea, then addressed the patient.

'Good evening,' he said quietly.

Dr. Barber did not expect a reply. One of the earliest phases of the experiment had involved removing the patient's tongue. In due course he'd also found it necessary to sever the patient's vocal chords. This had, ironically, made the insulating foam almost entirely redundant, although some sessions had still been a little on the noisy side. It was good to know the foam was there.

The patient lay on the table in the centre of the room. The saline drip, antibiotic drip and feeding tube were all in place. Above him on the ceiling, around the fierce light which shone into his face night and day, were photographs. All the photographs Dr. Barber had of them. He'd gathered them all up before the experiment began, from every shelf and album in the house, and affixed them to the ceiling above the table. It was an essential part of the experiment that the patient should never, even for a second, forget why he was here.

The patient was conscious, Dr. Barber was pleased to notice. He took the phial from the paper bag and studied it.

'I have something new for you today,' he said. The patient did not react. 'It wasn't easy to get hold of it, actually. It's illegal in many countries. It's used in executions, you see.'

The first reaction. The patient twitched and bucked against his restraints. Dr. Barber was irritated to notice that the contact abrasions on the patient's wrists were festering a little. He would adjust the antibiotic dose accordingly.

'Now don't get excited, you're not getting the full dose,' he said. 'In any event, this is only one of the drugs they use. First,' said Dr. Barber, drawing some of the drug into a syringe, 'the condemned man is given a general anaesthetic. It's more for the witnesses' benefit than the prisoner's, really.' Dr. Barber attached the syringe to the canula, which was permanently inserted into the back of the patient's fingerless hand.

'Once the prisoner is unconscious,' Dr. Barber went on, in the same soothing tone he used for his patients in the hospital, 'this second drug is administered. It's a powerful vascular irritant.'

Dr. Barber applied just the tiniest pressure to the syringe's plunger.

'The full dose – the lethal dose,' said Dr. Barber, 'will stop the prisoner's heart in seconds. A smaller dose, such as this, will simply cause severe irritation to the membranes of the blood vessels. It should feel,' he whispered into the patient's ear, 'like your blood is on fire.'

The drug began its journey around the patient's bloodstream. He twitched. He spasmed. He writhed. The rattling noise which was the closest thing he could make to a scream issued from his throat.

Nearly three and a half years into the experiment, it was getting harder and harder for Dr. Barber to find new techniques to employ. He was pleased to see that this one was proving effective.

He pulled up a chair, sat down, sipped his tea, and watched.

It was just over five years since the patient had entered

Dr. Barber's life. At sixty-two miles per hour, in a thirty zone, according to the police report.

Dr. Barber had been at the hospital when he heard about the accident, although he still refused to think of it as an accident. When a man drinks four pints of lager and three double whiskies and then gets behind the wheel of a Jaguar XF, what happens afterwards is not an accident. It's an atrocity.

At the joint funeral for his wife and daughter, Dr. Barber had not cried. His anger blunted his grief.

He'd attended the patient's trial, against the advice of his friends. No good can come of it, they'd said. But they'd been wrong.

During those numbing, empty months between the death of his family and the trial, he had been adrift, despairing, without hope or purpose. But in that courtroom, he had found a new reason to live.

He'd sat through the details of the incident: how the patient had gone drinking straight from work with his colleagues, how these colleagues had done nothing to dissuade him from driving home (none of them was on trial, for some reason which would always elude Dr. Barber), how he'd 'lost control' of his Jaguar (had he ever had control?) and crossed into oncoming traffic. The Jaguar had hit the little Fiat in which his wife had been bringing his daughter home from football practice, and . . .

He'd heard the description of their injuries, he was sure. But he'd never managed to recall them in any detail. Curious. But irrelevant.

Dr. Barber *did* recall the moment that the judge passed sentence. There had been statements from character witnesses as to how this had been an aberration, a one-off, a momentary and tragic lapse in judgment. The patient's work colleagues – the same ones who'd cheerfully watched him climb drunk into the driving seat – filed through the court in their best city pinstripes, painting a picture of a good and conscientious man who would be scarred forever by this tragedy. Like he was the victim.

When the judge pronounced the words 'two years' it had been all Dr. Barber could do not to laugh.

That was not the moment that Dr. Barber found a new purpose in life.

That came a few moments later, as the patient was led away to begin his pitiful sojourn of a sentence. He'd exchanged smiles of relief with his suited friends in the public gallery, and then his eyes had met Dr. Barber's.

And he winked.

He *winked*.

In that moment, both the course of the patient's life and the course of Dr. Barber's life were set irrevocably.

The plan had already begun to form in Dr. Barber's mind before he'd reached the bottom of the courthouse steps.

His own life, he knew, would henceforth consist of just one thing. Pain.

From waking each morning, to falling asleep each night, even in his dreams, he would know nothing but pain, and regret.

And as he replayed that cheerful wink over and over in his mind, Dr. Barber decided that pain and regret would be all that the patient would ever know, for the rest of his long, long life.

Much as Dr. Barber had expected, the patient behaved

himself impeccably in the ludicrous health spa-cum-country club which was the closest thing men of his up-bringing ever came to actual prison, and as such he was eligible for release after just twelve months. This had been ample time to prepare for him.

The abduction itself had been the most difficult part, but thanks to Dr. Barber's immaculate planning it went without a hitch.

He'd lured the patient to a private members' club on the pretence of being a tabloid newspaper reporter, eager to hear his side of the story, for which he would, of course, be paid handsomely. The patient's extremely well-paid job had *not* been kept vacant for him, and Dr. Barber suspected – rightly – that as a man of expensive tastes, he'd be keen to explore ways of making some quick and easy money.

When the patient arrived, he'd been shown to a booth near the front door of the club, where he found a glass of excellent single malt whisky (the same brand he'd been drinking on that day) and a note from the 're-porter', apologising for running late, and explaining that he'd called the club and ordered him a drink to enjoy while he was waiting.

From the far corner of the bar, Dr. Barber watched the patient read the note and drink the whisky.

The Rohypnol kicked in after about five minutes.

Dr. Barber helped the glassy-eyed, disorientated patient to his feet, apologised to the club staff for his friend's drunkenness and steered him out into the car park. The Jaguar was there, and the keys were in the patient's pocket.

The Jaguar was found burnt out in a ditch by the side of

a country road a few days later. The charred body inside was buried with the patient's name. But the patient himself was alive, if not especially well.

It hadn't been easy smuggling the poor young unidentified homeless man's body out of the hospital morgue two months previously, or indeed hauling it into the chest freezer Dr. Barber had installed in his garage for the very purpose of receiving it, some ten months earlier. Dr. Barber had been starting to worry that a suitable cadaver would not become available in time, but at no stage had he contemplated going out and taking one for himself. He wasn't a killer. Nobody would receive any treatment at his hands that they didn't richly deserve.

No one noticed that the immolated body behind the wheel of the Jaguar was that of a man a good ten years younger than the patient, or that it was half an inch too short, or that its teeth didn't match the patient's dental records. When a powerful car belonging to a man with a drink-driving conviction is found crashed and burnt out with a dead body in the driving seat, no one troubles the pathologist for a cause of death or a formal identification. Everyone can see what's happened.

By the time of the patient's opulent and well-attended funeral, the experiment had already been underway for a week. Dr. Barber had started with the patient's fingers and toes. He'd borrowed or filched the surgical equipment from the hospital. The bolt cutters he'd bought with his own money.

DAY 1,272

Dr. Barber checked on the patient before leaving for

work in the morning as he always did. The saline drip and feeding tube needed to be changed at least every forty-eight hours.

The patient had still been writhing and hissing in agony when Dr. Barber had turned in for the night. By the morning, the exotic execution drug seemed to have worn off. The patient was immobile, his eyes shut, his breath rasping.

'Good morning,' said Dr. Barber, holding the smelling salts to the patient's nostrils. The patient's eyes snapped open, red, staring. Dr. Barber had occasionally contemplated removing his eyelids, but he knew that this would make blindness inevitable, and he needed the patient's vision intact. He pointed at a photograph of his daughter, directly above the patient's face.

'It's her birthday,' he said. The patient did not react. 'I wonder what I'd have been giving her today . . .'

Dr. Barber gazed wordlessly at the photo for a moment. Then he spoke again: 'There were so many things I was looking forward to giving her.'

The syringe was still attached to the canula. Dr. Barber picked it up.

'There's only one thing I can give her now,' he said to the patient, 'and it's this.'

He gave the syringe another gentle squeeze.

Much as he wanted to stay and watch, Dr. Barber had work to do. He ascended the ladder. The sound of the patient's convulsing and wheezing was cut off by the closing hatch.

Dr. Barber was just breaking for lunch when his mobile rang. It was his next door neighbour. His burglar alarm was ringing, and since the highly expensive alarm system – selected by his wife shortly after they'd bought the place – was linked directly to the police station, there were now police cars in front of his house.

Police. At his house.

Dr. Barber furiously replayed the morning's events in his mind. He'd visited the patient, re-administered the drug, climbed the ladder, closed the hatch . . . Had he put the carpet back into place?

He couldn't remember.

He remembered closing the hatch, he remembered leaving the house, he remembered walking to the station, getting on the train into town . . . He did not remember replacing the carpet.

He didn't remember *not* replacing it, but nor did he remember replacing it.

He checked his watch. He had an hour. If he caught a cab he could make it home in twenty minutes . . . just time to let the police in, check the carpet, make them some tea, make his excuses and leave. Dr. Barber ran down the front steps of the hospital. There would usually be taxis queueing at the stand across the street, waiting for emerging patients and relatives. He saw that there was just one cab there.

Dr. Barber ran across the street. He had to catch that cab. If someone else nabbed it first then all would be lost. He waved to the driver as he ran. He saw the driver acknowledge his wave.

He didn't see the Ford Focus that hit him.

DAY 1,285

Dr. Barber's first thought was that he was thirstier than

he could ever remember being. He croaked a request for water; the nurse brought him some and then hurried to tell his doctor that he was awake.

Dr. Barber listened in silence as his doctor listed his injuries. His legs had escaped surprisingly more or less intact apart from some severe bruising; he'd badly dislocated his left shoulder on the car's bonnet then shattered the elbow of the other arm when he threw it up in front of his face as he was thrown to the tarmac. This had reduced the force with which his head had hit the road just enough to save his life. He was lucky, his doctor told him, to have escaped with a severe concussion. In the meantime, he was to take it easy; after nearly two weeks of unconsciousness it would take him a while to regain his faculties.

Nearly two weeks.

His neighbour visited him the next day; the police had checked the exterior of the house, and, finding all the doors and windows still closed and locked, they'd called the security company and told them to chalk it up as a false alarm. Some of these new extra-sensitive systems could be set off by things like cats jumping over garden walls or birds flying into windows, apparently. There had been nothing to worry about.

Nothing to worry about.

Dr. Barber, his right elbow in plaster, was discharged two days later. He'd been away from the house for fifteen days.

He paid the cab driver and shuffled painfully up the drive to the front door. He had to reach into his right pocket with his left hand to retrieve his keys. The residual pain in his recently dislocated shoulder made this an uncomfortable task.

Dr. Barber opened the front door and looked down at the floor of his hall.

He had, in fact, put the carpet back in place that morning.

He entered the house, painfully removed his jacket and hung it on the bannister. He took a few steps forward and stared at the slit in the carpet.

He already knew what he would find down there. But he still had to check.

Dr. Barber knelt stiffly and peeled back the carpet. He twisted the brass ring with his left hand and pulled. The weight of the hatch sent spasms of pain through his shoulder, but he succeeded in hauling it open.

The smell hit him immediately.

Dr. Barber climbed awkwardly down the ladder, and, wincing, pulled the hatch closed to contain the foul odour.

It was impossible to tell what had killed the patient: dehydration from the exhausted saline drip was the most likely culprit, followed by starvation from the empty feeding tube; possibly septicaemia from the festering abrasions at his wrists and ankles. It would have been painful, in any event. Some scant consolation.

Dr. Barber would address himself to the problem of disposing of the body in due course. First he needed a cup of tea.

He climbed the ladder, and pushed against the hatch.

A bolt of pain surged through his arm and straight down his left side. Dr. Barber flinched, swayed, and fell from the ladder, landing painfully in a seated position.

He scrambled to his feet and climbed the ladder again. He tried to raise his left arm but it wouldn't respond. His right arm, still broken, was curled uselessly against his body. His left, meanwhile, refused to obey his brain.

With a superhuman effort, and sweating with agony, Dr. Barber hauled his left hand upwards to the hatch. He felt the smooth surface against his palm, but as he tried to push against it, searing, blinding pain coursed through him. He tried again. The pain intensified. The hatch did not budge. Dr. Barber collapsed, exhausted, at the foot of the ladder.

He'd seen, and treated, enough injuries like his own to be able to form a decent prognosis. The strength would not return to his left arm for at least two weeks; his broken right arm would be useless for twice that time.

Dr. Barber did not bother even contemplating calling out for help. The polyurethane would absorb his cries, and even if anyone were to hear, would he really want to be discovered in his cellar next to a mutilated and decomposing body?

The same problem would apply if he phoned for assistance, assuming he could get any signal in the insulated cellar . . . then Dr. Barber remembered that his phone was in the pocket of his jacket, hanging on the bannister, just a couple of metres away, on the other side of the immovable hatch.

Dr. Barber sat in the chair and looked at the purplish body of the patient on the table.

He sighed. It didn't matter now. The experiment was over. His work was done. His life and that of the patient had been inextricably enmeshed for five years, bonded forever in pain and remorse. It made perfect sense that they should remain together now. Without his patient to attend to, his life had no purpose anyway.

Dr. Barber scanned the shelves of the cellar. There were, he knew, instruments and substances there which he could use to hasten his own end. Perhaps he would do that in due course.

Or perhaps he'd just wait. He knew how to wait. He was patient.

AL MURRAY

FOR EVERYONE'S GOOD

THIS ROOM IS my room. It's been my room since I came here, when my stepmother decided enough was enough, that we had done all we could at home. My teeth hurt so much, I never once calmed of their pain, and she and my father couldn't stand my moaning, and father hated that it distracted me so I would not read. I came here when I may have been twenty-five, I may have been twenty-six, it is all so long ago and numbers were never clear to me nor friendly.

We came up the avenue; the trees are so tall now, they have had to cut some down to make room for how broad they have grown; there are bumps where the stumps were, like tree echoes. The trees I first saw when they were young like me, their leaves have come and gone more times than anyone could count, all those unfriendly numbers, and beyond the pond where some-times we would go to play with boats, always under the eye of the Coats – I called them Coats, did the others? Some of the others were children, I don't remember them so well, and I don't know where the others have gone now too – there is a low, grey building, and coloured carriages come and go all day. They sit in lines and wait all day. If a carriage can wait all day you must be very rich. Maybe it is a palace, or a zoo like the one in the park I went to with my sisters before I came here, though the animals must all be indoors.

Our carriage was black, though we had taken the new train that made my stepmother very nervous, and then taken the black carriage to the house. As the trees went past the window my stepmother, Mrs Evans (she took my father's name but I liked to call her Mrs Evans when the pain in my teeth and my busy thoughts let me speak) did not look me in the eye. She had not looked me in the eye since the train left London. She often looked at the floor, the wall, my pinny, rather than look at me. When she spoke, and said my name, it was as if she was talking about someone else, or something she could not hold.

My mother held me but she had died when I was still a baby, so Mr Evans, my father, said. We would try to read together, and he would begin patiently always, until his patience had dripped out of him like the last drops of tea in a pot, and the air around him would ache, his shoulder would sink and he would sigh, deep, unhappy sighs. I would sigh too and I would try harder to read, to speak, to say I understood, but my teeth hurt, and my stomach would grind and I would feel him push me away even by doing nothing. I still want to read, but books seem of another world now, an old world, my father's world that sent me away.

Mrs Evans took me up the stairs here at the house, and we were greeted kindly. She drank tea and talked to Dr Carter, a man with a kind face for strangers, a different face for everyone who had his acquaintance. Acquaintance: a word I could never see when it was in a book, the letters were not friendly. When Mrs Evans left, and hands had been shook, goodbye madam, goodbye doctor, sir, Dr Carter saw to it that my clothes were taken somewhere safe, so very safe they have not returned. And then one of the Coats came and cut my hair. I loved to brush my hair for calm and now that calm has gone.

The colourful chariots come and go from the zoo palace; they have lamps, the light swoops through the night. They brought me to this room, and although the view has changed, and although the Coats no longer come, days remain the same, followed by nights. No one comes to bring me food anymore, but that means no one raps my knuckles when I won't eat, it means that Dr Harold Carter or Dr Martlett Trevelyan or Dr James Grey who was married to Dr Martlett Trevelyan's daughter Eliza won't raise their voices any more, bind my hands, scrub my teeth with the wire brush, no one pours the cold water on my back, no one shouts at me when I cannot find the words, or will not play their games, or sing along, or drink my tonic that grips my tummy.

And Mrs Evans, my stepmother, she doesn't come to see me, she came only twice. The second time she came her eyes said goodbye, but like when I got stuck with a word reading with father, the words would not come out of her mouth. I said what I knew, I said I know you won't see me again, and I pulled at my hair, and I wept more tears, the kind that do not work, not like my sisters' tears which can get you all sorts of things, but not out of this house and home.

Mr Evans, my sisters' father now I suppose, no longer mine, never did come to see me. We stopped reading together long before the train came to take me – did we take the train to come here to the house? The air would ache all around him. He would close the door, and he and Mrs Evans would talk behind the door, and he would shout sometimes surely to make sure that I heard him through the door, and while they would never say my name I think they talked of me. I know they talked of me. 'What shall we do, Larissa? Our daughters cannot have this distraction as they grow older! This can only corrupt, damage their lives. One so, so feeble of mind.'

Mrs Evans would reply: 'But Charles, what does compassion dictate?' This was Mrs E's – yes, I know my alphabet thank you to Alice the Coat – favourite word, a word that she only said when deciding what to do with me. 'Com-passion' what can it mean? My sisters played upstairs, Emily reading to Tess, reading so well Mr Evans would say, reading like they were born to it. Reading like it was their nature. Reading like their family would read.

One day that conversation included Dr Carter, Dr Harold Carter ABCDEFG, whose coach was a very dark rose red. His coach waited, he wore a gold watch and chain, and he could use the watch to decide what time it was. I like to tell the time for myself, clock faces say so little. Dr Carter closed the door but did not shout, so I do not know what he said, though it is all so long ago I could not remember it well enough even if I could recall. It was one of their talks about com-passion and they decided I am sure for the train to come and take me to the carriage and trees going past on either side. I pushed my ear to the keyhole and told myself be quiet and wait! I am quite wrong, I can remember though I might not understand.

Dr Harold Carter says: 'The girl is no longer a girl, she is a woman now, yet still a child. But now lives as a woman who, if allowed to have offspring of her own, may add further to this world's woes.' The world's woes now? Are mine not enough? I think but I have to be quiet and cannot understand. 'It is our moral duty, and a duty of compassion' – com-passion, com-passion, com-passion is here to decide again – 'to your late wife's daughter, and to society itself, the body of the nation, to ensure her care takes place somewhere where she, and no other, can come to harm. It is your and our moral imperative. For everyone's good' and with those words I stopped being quiet, and cried more useless tears and my teeth they hurt and I scratched my gums until Mrs Evans, her face in thunder, sadder than the sighs my father gave when I spilt my soup and wailed because it was hot on my legs, took me to my room past my reading sisters and to my bed. And the air in the whole house moaned and I sang with it and I wished that I could read the way they wanted me to, and that for once my teeth and tummy did not hurt and that com-passion would go away.

And many years later, many years after Dr Martlett Trevelyan who never spoke of com-passion had said as if I could not hear that I had no family beyond these walls. And I would sleep long days and nights, days and nights would come and go as they always do. And I had slept for so long that day that no longer did the dreams about my sister coming bother me. I had heard the Coats talk about her, the woman who wrote books, and I was her sister, the girl who could not look at them with the air starting to ache as it had around Mr Evans. I was her sister, that is why they talked about me, I was her sister. Her books. Her books were books that, so said the Coats, everyone was reading. She had become they said 'quite famous really – but they're not the kind of books I ever read, Mary' they said to me. The world knew who she was, and would remember her maybe, but she had forgotten me, Emily Evans had forgotten me.

I had slept so long that Dr Harold Carter no longer came, that the trees had grown as tall as the house and the palace had grown beyond the lake. A long time I was alone in the house, but now there are new people in my room. They are like Mr and Mrs Evans though I never did hear Mr and Mrs E speak of love to one another so. And they do not like books, they do not like to read, they sit and watch pictures on the wall where my chair would lean and Alice would sit and sing and brush my hair sometimes and bring me calm. Mr Evans would not like them not at all, and Mrs Evans would have to show her com-passion again: they do not read! But Mr Evans will not come to visit them ever, for it would mean he would need to come and see me and it is for everyone's good that he does not, and surely mine most of all. And so I sit beside the sofa, and brush my hair, and watch this man and this woman as they seem to live here by themselves and in the room next door where they sleep. No doctors come, no Coats. All is calm. My teeth no longer hurt, though sometimes in other rooms I hear the air begin to moan and cannot help myself and I moan as well. The man and the woman don't like this, he tells her it is the wind blowing through the building and she calms down but maybe he knows it's more. If I moan perhaps they will remember me. And he did see me once, me whom no one cared to see, he caught my eye, and did not look away the way my family did, at least not right away.

This room is my room, and it has been my room since my stepmother decided enough was enough. She has not come to take me home, and I will wait until she does.

MARY EVANS, daughter of the writer and explorer CHARLES EVANS and his first wife MARY (née CLEMENT) and sister of the novelist EMILY EVANS (*The Church of Glass*, *Buttermore Farm*) died of pneumonia in November 1946, having outlived her more famous family. She died in the room she had first been assigned to upon being committed at the famous Dunswood Hall Asylum for the Feeble Minded and Imbecile in Sussex under Dr H. Carter in 1899. Miss EVANS' funeral was unattended.

STEWART LEE

A VIEW FROM A HILL

A CHRISTMAS GHOST STORY

I ARRESTED MR Lee at 7 a.m. this morning as an accessory to multiple charges of arson, assault and grievous bodily harm. I have received confirmation from Scotland Yard that he will spend the festive season in the cells, with no possibility of bail. Mr Lee used his one phone call to contact his wife, who, he said, was furious that he was now unlikely to make it to his brother-in-law's by the evening of the 24th. Amusingly, he claimed this was the only good thing to come out of the whole affair. I laughed, but I have just heard that he is a 'comedian', so I am no longer impressed by his ability to make light of the situation, and feel that what seemed a special moment between us was, for Mr Lee, just business as usual. Nonetheless, Mr Lee maintains, with some degree of certainty, that this is, on balance, his worst Christmas to date.

DETECTIVE INSPECTOR
MONTAGUE R. JAMES, 24/12/12

My best Christmas was 1988, though it wasn't strictly Christmas. It was December 21st, the winter solstice. But as my companion that evening, Julian Fullsome-Swathe, explained, the 21st had always been the date of Christmas until someone moved the calendar by four days. He couldn't remember who exactly, but it was three in the morning and we were some distance into our second Thermos flask of magic mushroom tea, which made all notions of the measurement of time seem rather slippery. Julian and I were undergraduates in our final year at Oxford. He was top public school stock and stiff-uppered military background, going back centuries, and lower middle-class forelock-tugger. But I liked Julian, and was genetically and socially predestined to serve him.

In recent months, Julian had become intent on pursuing various experiences which, he explained darkly, he would never be able to enjoy subsequently due to the secretive career path on which he had chosen to embark after graduation. This was Oxford in the eighties: our elderly English professor was romantically rumoured to be a talent scout for the intelligence services, and Julian was perfect state-assassin material. And now, in the final months before the black cloud of unknowing that he was entering finally and fully enveloped him, I was leading him along a wintry Wiltshire Ridgeway by starlight, aglow on psilocybins I'd purchased from the didgeridoo player who lived in a converted ambulance in the public car park at Port Meadow.

High above the Ock valley we scrabbled through the Iron Age undulations of the White Horse hillfort until we beheld through a light frosting of fresh fallen snow, the elegant flanks of the prehistoric hill figure itself, four hundred feet of chalk, flourished outlines hugging the graceful curves of the upland, a view as close to a holy vision as a confirmed agnostic like myself might ever achieve, and one of the few sights that still stirs in me troubling twinges of the scoundrel patriotism.

Then, as now, I fancied myself a keen folklorist, and my study bedroom was littered with dusty tomes. I explained, breathlessly, to Julian that the horse might commemorate King Alfred's 871AD victory over the Danes at the Battle of Ashdown; or date back 3,000 years to the later Bronze Age; or have been formed when the ground was stained by the very blood of the dragon Saint George was said to have slain. The state of mind we were in, all three explanations seemed equally probable.

'They say that if England is threatened, the horse will rise up from the hill and take revenge,' I said. Julian, who had come prepared, was now cranking out his favourite childhood song, Jackie Lee's theme from the 1965 Yugoslavian children's TV series *The White Horses*, from a scratched 7-inch single on a vintage portable Dansette. 'The White Horse is rising, Stewart,' he said. 'Can't you see it?'

Even before my arrest, Christmas 2012 hadn't been going well. I'm a stand-up comedian for a living. I cope reasonably well with the job itself. It's the promotional duties I find degrading. I have a stand-up DVD available for purchase, *Carpet Remnant World*, which has sat as a non-mover at number twelve in the Amazon charts for two months now. Viewed as a niche art–comedy turn, I can't afford to supply my product to supermarkets at a cheap enough price per unit to make them stock it; panel show promotional opportunities don't work for an act as lugubrious as mine; and whenever I am interviewed I manage to say something ill-considered which, when decontextualised by Jan Moir, makes for a minor *Daily Mail* horror story, to the understandable embarrassment of friends and relations.

To show willing to my financial backers, I usually spend the months surrounding the release dates of my work writing supposedly amusing think pieces, appended with DVD details, for liberal broadsheet newspapers. Their readerships comprise, for better or worse, my key audience, and I attempt assiduously to maintain their loyalty, and their respect, by flattering their intelligence, while simultaneously insulting their core moral and political values. So far this December I have compared John Cage to Ant and Dec in the *Guardian* and, in the *Observer*, I have drawn spurious parallels between David Cameron's *News of the World* text messages and Shakespeare, between *I'm a Celebrity . . . . Get Me Out of Here!* and Kafka's *Metamorphosis*, and Edgar Rice Burroughs's *Tarzan* and Michael Gove's education policies. I have a simple and repetitive comic formula, which I despatch in the voice of a semi-fictional version of myself.

This year my publicist had been uncharacteristically keen that I write a piece for a magazine called *ShortList*, which is given away free on the street to passers-by and offers expert advice on style and fitness, the latest in films, gaming, culture and technology to time-poor young professionals in search of an off-the-peg identity they haven't earned. I doubted that anyone that liked my work would read it, and tried to wriggle out of her request, but our financial backers were keen for me to ensnare the lucrative male grooming market, and it was agreed that I would submit to *ShortList* an amusing, 1,000-word, end-of-year round-up of things I hated about 2012.

I arrogantly imagined I could complete this assignment in such a way as satisfied *ShortList*'s editors while also maintaining the trademark subversion of media tropes my regular customer base has come to expect from me. The deadline was Thursday 13 December and I was due to file a Christmas story for the *New Statesman* four days later, a deal which had been arranged by the comedian–scientist Robin Ince. Despite being chiefly responsible for our two small children due to my wife's current professional ambitions, I imagined I could easily complete both in time. The *ShortList* piece would take me five or six minutes, the *New Statesman* story a week at least.

That evening, Monday 10 December, my stepfather rang me from the Worcestershire village where he lives, saying he thought he had seen my old university friend Julian sitting on the pavement outside the second-hand bookshop in Malvern, crying. I believed him. I had seen Julian in the same place, in the same state, nine years ago, dishevelled and grey, the haunted look that had first appeared on his face that night at the White Horse more pronounced than ever.

We went for a drink. Things had not gone well for Julian, evidently, but he wouldn't say exactly why. Many different and admittedly melodramatic explanations suggested themselves in my subconscious. The SAS had originally been garrisoned at nearby Malvern Wells, GCHQ employed thousands of spooks down the road at Cheltenham, and in the fifties and sixties, Powick Hospital, not far away en route to Worcester, dosed thousands of unwitting patients with LSD. Local pub backroom folklore regularly tied these strands together, leading to the assumption that any wild-eyed vagrant drifting through the region was some former intelligence services insider whose brain had been wiped clean out of political necessity by ruthless government scientists. Was it melodramatic to assume that Julian himself had perhaps done something in the service of the Crown that was now deemed best forgotten?

Sadly, it would pain me too much to detail Julian's paranoid ramblings in full. I'm sorry to say the White Horse, and especially its legendary and vengeful coming to life, loomed large in all of them. The fact that I must have felt a degree of responsibility for this is borne out by my taking him immediately to the cashpoint and giving him everything I had in my account, in those pre-DVD deal days of the early noughties a sorry £260. Heartbreakingly, Julian then dragged me to a large puddle near the former Winter Gardens, insisted it was Malvern spring water, bubbling up out of the earth, and demanded that I join him in lapping it up. I drank as much of the muddy mixture as I could stand, but Julian no longer inspired in me the loyalty he once did, and I left him there licking alone.

The *ShortList* piece proved more difficult to pull off than I had patronisingly imagined. I had hoped to pastiche punchy lad-mag style and twist it to my own ends, but there's a headbutt economy about gadget porn that's actually hard to approximate, and one learns a grudging respect for it when trying to mimic it. My idea was to list ten things that had disappointed me in 2012, avoiding the usual celebrity and automobile-based value judgements a typical *ShortList* contributor might usually finger, and to use instead specific incidents from the year to establish, point by point, a portrait of a general existential despair that would subversively stun *ShortList* readers stumbling across it by accident. And I almost got away with it.

I began writing the *ShortList* anti-review of the year on the morning of the 13th by complaining about the Irish bookmakers Paddy Power. In March, the gambling business had, without permission from the National Trust who manage the site, mounted a massive picture of a jockey overnight on the back of the White Horse of Uffington, driving pegs into its prehistoric surface, in order to promote their betting outlets at the Cheltenham Festival race meeting. Paddy Power desecrated what is a religious site, or a work of art, or both, in the name of grubby commerce, and then treated anyone who objected as if they were a humourless curmudgeon. 'I hope everyone who works for Paddy Power, or thought this was funny, is fucked to death by a giant white horse, the cold-hearted sport morons,' I concluded, lads'-mag style.

Then I took aim at James Dyson, who I called the inventor of 'the wanker's Hoover', for describing teenagers interested in arts and culture as fools 'going off to study French lesbian poetry. I hope Dyson's millionaire penis will be torn off in the suckpipe of one of his own Hoovers, a fate that would never befall a French lesbian poet.' But a call from my daughter's nursery reporting sickness and loose bowels meant I had to collect her early, and I spent the rest of the day caring for her. My son returned from school in a similar state, and I was unable to resume writing until both had fallen finally and fitfully asleep at around 11 p.m.

From the initial two examples of crass, philistine attitudes – Paddy Power and Dyson – I then worked through various others, including the shared houses on my Hackney street with filthy front gardens piled with rubbish, all full of young, middle-class trustafarians temporarily holidaying in other people's actual neighbourhoods, each with the face 'of Jack Whitehall'; to a more specific disgust at the drug dealers who let their feral weapon dogs defecate outside my gate every night; and at the young man I watched urinating, at some length, into my doorway late one Saturday evening, when there are much more convenient walls and hedges all around; all of which seemed to me to be part of the same general contempt for basic human decency.

'It begins with Paddy Power shitting on the Uffington White Horse and ends with a man pissing on my house,' I concluded. 'I have hated 2012. I expect next year will be worse.' I finally filed the piece twelve hours late, at 4 a.m., my work delayed by stomach bugs my children had doubtless picked up from the human and animal urine and excrement smeared around the front door of their home. I bet my publicist a nominal wager the piece would be rejected by *ShortList*.

The next morning, having got the children to school and nursery, I went back to bed until 11, intending to begin on the *New Statesman* Christmas story. But my publicist woke me with a call to tell me that *ShortList* liked the piece so much they wanted an extra 200 words, comprising a further two entries, making a top twelve of things I'd hated in 2012. I set to work, not a little bemused, if inconvenienced, and then all my old alarm bells rang. Presumably, *ShortList* could see the piece worked as a whole, and weren't just trying to fillet it into fragments, with one section substituted for another? Or were they covertly trying to cut sections and getting me to write replacement paragraphs without telling me?

My publicist asked them directly, and the predictably disheartening reply arrived.

'Sorry I wasn't clear. We were actually hoping for two replacement entries as a couple of the subjects Stewart has tackled will be problematic for us to get into the mag. We've got commercial business planned with both Paddy Power and Dyson, so these are the two we'd be looking to replace with a few of Stewart's initial suggestions below to take it back up to 1,200 words. Also, given that he was on our cover a few weeks ago, is there another name we can use other than Jack Whitehall?'

But that night on the White Horse with Julian a quarter of a century ago had meant a lot to me. It had been an epiphany of sorts, and I genuinely believed the hill figure to be an expression of the triumph of the human spirit and imagination. So I said I wouldn't be able to submit anything to *ShortList* after all. I was not prepared to be held hostage by Dyson, Paddy Power and Jack Whitehall. But my writing time for this *New Statesman* story had been seriously eaten into by the *ShortList* business; there was the not inconsiderable matter of two outstanding sets of infants' excrement- and vomit-stained sheets and blankets needing to be washed; and I had promised my stepfather I would go to Worcestershire that weekend to help him reposition an antique sundial.

It was late on the night of Friday 14 December when I finally began work on the *New Statesman* Christmas story, abandoning it only at 3 a.m., after a misguided and drunken attempt to retell the Nativity from the viewpoint of a sceptical shepherd, from which we have only this extract: 'Cows moo, sheep baa, baby, virgin, carpenter. A political manifesto in the form of a tableau. I know my Isaiah, that suffering servant shtick, and so does whoever went and stage-managed this.' It was going nowhere, and I needed the *New Statesman* gig to plug my DVD.

The next morning I bundled the sickly and protesting children into their car seats and set off for Worcestershire. A few miles short of my stepfather's I stopped at the Caffè Nero in Malvern for a coffee. The three of us sat around a window table, mainlining caffeine and fruit smoothies, and across the road in the graveyard of the 11th-century Priory I suddenly saw Julian, a decade worn and ragged, but Julian nonetheless. And he saw me. I beckoned him to join us and negotiated him into accepting a hot tomato and pasta-based dish.

Julian and I made awkward small talk while the children plastered stickers of Peppa Pig into Peppa Pig-shaped spaces in Peppa Pig comics. He told me about the Malvern Hills, the Herefordshire Beacon and the Iron Age hillfort, the Wyche Cutting, rich in salt, the winter sun over the frost, the view out towards Wales, and Clutter's Cave, where you could shelter and drink spring water from the cliff face. I told him about my DVD promotional obligations, and *ShortList* and Paddy Power, Dyson and Jack Whitehall. I remember that I said to him, 'Every single story connected to the White Horse is about fables of national identity in one way or another. Imagine if we went over to Ireland and painted a picture of Oliver Cromwell on to the front of the Newgrange burial chamber and then tried to make out it was a bit of fun.' In the light of what was to happen, this idiotic imperialist joke was a flippant comment that I bitterly regret. Who knows where Julian had been serving, and what part of our now politically awkward British imperial history his actions may have been written out of? Did I trigger something?

My stepfather's sundial could wait. Over a second festive gingerbread-flavoured caffè latte, Julian and I laughed about how our lives couldn't have been more different. He said he appreciated how, when we last met, I had given him everything I had, and said he'd repay the favour one day. Even utterly destitute, he still gave off that refined sense of minor aristocratic decency, as if I was in his debt, as if he were the high-status figure. My almost-two-year-old daughter registered Julian's innate superiority, immediately stared at him intently through-out our encounter, a little in love, and then watched him silently as he strode off back through the grave-stones, his military bearing at odds with his dishevelled appearance.

As I drove on to my stepfather's, I remembered that night on White Horse Hill, twenty-four years ago. Ju-lian had said the White Horse was rising. And, as he watched, it was. Slowly, as snowflakes caught in the star-light, the equine figure shook itself free of the turf, and stood, and stamped its feet. Then it turned, snorted, and fixed Julian's gaze for a full minute or so with its baleful opal eyes. 'The White Horse,' he whispered, tugging at my sleeve. And I saw him as he saw it leap up through the snow and out into the stars, its hooves beating rip-ples into the black velvet fabric of the famished night. But I didn't see the horse myself. Only Julian did. And as he watched the White Horse canter across the face of the moon, he turned and gripped me tightly by the shoulder, suddenly and irrevocably changed: 'If, in the future, Stewart, you should ever need anyone eliminated, and without a paper trail that connects to you, come and find me. That's all I can say.' Then he turned away. 'Now watch that White Horse fly.'

I finally filed the *New Statesman* Christmas story dreadfully late in the day on 17 December, having taken the venerable magazine's deadline to the wire. In the end, I decided to use my personal experience of the transfiguration of Julian Fullsome-Swathe and the solstice vision of the White Horse as a metaphor for all that is true and pure, and my struggles to write about Paddy Power and the White Horse for *ShortList* as examples of all that is vulgar and base, with the implication that the 'White Horse' of my own work, namely the *Carpet Remnant World* stand-up comedy DVD, was similarly contaminated by contact with the world of commerce. I don't know if it really worked, but pin-eyed from late-night cycles of coffee and wine, I took the afternoon of the 18th off and then resolved to spend the next week planning for Christmas. That afternoon, Robin Ince told me the *New Statesman* had chosen not to run the story, and was going to fill the space with a hastily scribbled cartoon of the late MP Cyril Smith as Father Christmas that folded out over two double spreads. And, three days later, on 21 December, the atrocities began.

Eighty-eight branches of Paddy Power were fire-bombed during the small hours of the morning of 21 December, and the business's chief executives Patrick Kennedy and Cormac McCarthy both woke to find the severed heads of white horses next to them in bed; eighty-eight dead white horses, their genitals horribly mutilated, were left on the doorsteps of eighty-eight branches of Debenhams, whose chairman, Nigel Northridge, is also a non-executive director of Paddy Power; James Dyson awoke to find himself bound with the flex of a Dyson cleaner, his home surrounded by dozens of Dysons, somehow modified to broadcast, through the apertures of their distinctive suck funnels, readings of the works of Renée Vivien and Natalie Barney: 'My brunette with the golden eyes, your ivory body, your amber/Has left bright reflections in the room/Above the garden./The clear midnight sky, under my closed lids/Still shines . . . I am drunk from so many roses/Redder than wine.' And passers-by, silenced by the beauty, cursed the cold-hearted inventor. And somewhere in Knightsbridge, Jack Whitehall, newly crowned British Comedy Awards King of Comedy, opens his eyes to find his childhood pet hamster eviscerated, and paper crowns smeared with dog excrement hung around the eaves of his penthouse apartment. When the news of these crimes broke, an efficient *New Statesman* sub-editor remembered my rejected story and contacted the police

What I found difficult to understand, having checked Mr Lee's college records, was that the Julian he wrote about appears not to have existed at all, as if he fabricated the character in his New Statesman *Christmas story for some reason to which only he was privy. Apart from that, our investigations show that the details of every other part of Mr Lee's story are entirely, even uncannily, accurate.*

DETECTIVE INSPECTOR
MONTAGUE R. JAMES, 26/12/12

ROBIN INCE

MOST OUT OF CHARACTER

THE SCREAMING WAS deafening.

The panic was swollen-eyed and chaotic.

Whatever it was had startled them from their brain-stem instincts into a very conscious terror. He had been told that intelligence was what you used when you didn't know what to do, a relief from the binary options that most animals are stuck with.

Like that frog he'd seen that had its eyes turned upside down by some scientist investigating whatever it was that scientists investigate when they feel the need to turn a frog's eyes upside down. That stupid frog, every time a fly flew by its tongue would go in the opposite direction, down, not up.

Stupid, stupid frog.

It got hungrier and hungrier, but it never learnt.

He wasn't that keen on vivisection, after all, he was a vegetarian, he had been since he saw Morrissey for the first time. He had a morbid fear of meeting Morrissey and smelling of mince or bacon, so had stuck by his principles, though he did sometimes eat foie gras.

He hated those vegetarians who felt all guilty because they had a bit of chicken or tuna; if you are going to break the rules, really break the rules.

Lose your willpower and eat something that exploded inside a duck, or was it a goose?

He couldn't remember.

He could kill a fly, but he couldn't kill a bee. They danced. If an animal has learnt a complex series of dance moves to express itself, then let it live.

But flies?

To hell with flies.

Who cares?

Why get teary over a fly.

That silly human trait of anthropomorphising.

The fly has no inner life, he thought. It's not as if it gets hit by a newspaper and falls to its death ruing that it was a bitter irony that today of all days he died, his day of retirement, the last day that he was to vomit on ham before moving to the Algarve to spend his splendid last days shitting on cheese.

What was all this screaming about? It was beginning to annoy him. That laughable foolishness of panic that sledgehammers the veneer of human sophistication.

'I am not an animal?'

Of course you were, Joseph Merrick.

We all are, whether we have bumpy, lumpy heads or aqualine noses and alluring eyes.

He didn't like being an animal. He liked politeness and wine and talking about impenetrable books that won prizes. He controlled his urges. He was meticulous, most of the time. Perhaps very late at night he would let himself go a little, he might peer at what others were doing and experience the vicarious thrill of others' lust slowly bleeding into his own, but he was never seedy.

Another scream pierced him. He had a sense of looking up, though numb and blurry. He was seeing everything as if it was surrounded by a heat haze. Slightly disembodied, like that time he had half-wittedly bought those 'legal highs' from the back of a magazine of ghosts, leprechauns and water memory. He wouldn't do that again. It had taken almost a fortnight to get possession of his body back. He had sat stiffly in an armchair for days, looking at his own hands, perplexed by the movement of his own fingers. Had he met his homunculus? He felt a little like that now, he wasn't even sure where his hands were . . . or his feet. Not only was he not feeling himself, he really couldn't feel himself. Did he feel dizzy? Was he lost? Did he feel sick or well?

The square was empty now, though he saw it before him, he didn't know for sure if he was in it. In the distance, a man ran into the square, saw something, and ran, startled. Everyone else was scared, why wasn't he?

What had the man seen that he hadn't or couldn't?

He saw a hand.

It was his hand.

And it was bloody.

Sodden with gore.

He felt real emotion now. He had felt passive, but now he was panicked too, like those silly, screeching droves that had flailed and yelped through the square just moments ago.

This fear was very different to their haphazard emoting.

He wondered if he was the cause of it all. If that red

hand was his, was he dying, or even dead? Had he been brutally slaughtered and now his torn corpse was the source of terror?

Was this what dying felt like, an ebbing away of awareness? Where was he going?

He looked again, his hand was still moving, so he was still alive. It wasn't merely moving, it was moving wildly. When he first observed it he had thought it was still, a trick of the mind, it was reaching into something.

Not just reaching, tearing.

And his other hand too.

His hands were in offal, steaming offal.

His hands were in the pit of a stomach, wildly pulling.

This was disgusting.

He was pulling at the tubes, red meat, and putty of something.

He should stop that right away, this was quite out of character.

He instructed his hands to stop, he urged them to desist, but they wouldn't obey him.

Had he confused his hands for someone else's?

Was he the victim? Maybe he had confused his hands for those of the madman who was slaughtering him?

But only if the slaughterer had the same signet ring as him.

No, these were his hands.

And they weren't just tearing into something, they were bringing the raw lumps to his mouth. He would have felt sick, but he didn't seem able to.

He was revolting.

He tried to close his mouth, to seal his lips, to stop the steaming lumps making it inside him.

Urgh, this looked like a bit of pancreas.

This was uncouth.

Uncouth?

It was more than bloody uncouth, he was leaning over someone, he knew it was a person now, immersed in their guts. This had definitely never happened before. He once killed a bird with a stone, but he was very young and he was only trying to help. It was a wren that had damaged itself in some wire. He wrapped it in tissue paper then repeatedly struck it. There was no hidden joy, no vicarious thrill. It was the only way he could think of killing it, twisting its neck would have been too visceral, too real.

This was real.

God, when was he going to stop, ripping and tearing and shovelling, what a nasty brute.

Most out of character.

The body was nearly empty now.

He saw the face above it, mauled and vacuous.

It was Lucas.

He didn't like Lucas. He was in PR.

But he had never imagined beating him to death and eating his entrails.

He really was an arsehole, but if you cannibalised all the arseholes in the world, you'd be exhausted and plagued by peptic ulcers.

Even though Lucas was now hollow, he didn't feel full. For a man with not much of an appetite, he thought he looked bloated. He had two sets of lungs, a second spleen and pretty much everything else inside him now, but he still didn't feel anything.

He saw himself getting up, but so clumsily. He was never clumsy. Posture had always been important, he'd even gone on a course and had his own yoga mat. To publicly stagger like a drunk was not to his liking. It was almost a relief that everyone had run away upon seeing the sight of him gorging on a dead man, it saved the shame of this display.

He had once seen someone at an outdoor festival who had lost the ability to co-ordinate his limbs. He was stuck on the ground, desperately trying to work out the sequencing of his legs, but to no avail. Someone had told him that the man was in a K-hole; apparently excessive ketamine use can obliterate your motor skills.

Perhaps that is what had happened. Someone had managed to spike him with ketamine and that is what had caused this whole damn mess. He saw Lucas below him.

No, that mess really was too big a side effect for some drugs, even those ones he had read about being used on soldiers in Vietnam.

He couldn't quite place where he was in his brain now, the himness of him seemed to be shifting. The ghost in the machine seemed to be thinning out.

He was fully standing now, upright and dripping. He was walking freely, a stiffness around the knees, but no longer lumbering. He thought he felt tired, but despite his desire to sit down, he walked past the bench with the small plaque for a Molly who 'always enjoyed this view, Died 2006. Much loved by Polly and Neil'. He didn't seem able to tell himself what to do.

A dog ran through the square.

A terrier.

He liked terriers, not so much he would run after one, but he was now.

He was chasing a small dog, he was running with an

urgency he had never experienced before, and he didn't like it.

It didn't take long to eat the dog. There was some vomiting: the hair had jammed in his throat and the automatic responses of his body had contracted and puked the tangled mess while he watched. What was he watching? Was he watching him, or was he him and this was it. He was beginning to accept he had become a puppet dictator of his own body, maybe he always had been. He didn't like it. He concentrated hard. He hoped to move his arm the way he wanted, like some charlatan psychic who has begun to believe he really can move teaspoons with his mind, but all the staring is to no avail.

He was leaning in the dark now, an alley filled with bin liners. Perhaps he was going to sleep.

The dream was comforting. He was civilised. He was frying tofu and ginger, he had never fried tofu and ginger in a dream before. In the dream he could smell the ginger. In the dream he ate with cutlery. In the dream he was vivacious. As the dawn light interfered with the dream, the fine meal ended with a brutal attack by wok, few survived.

He was awake and so was the thing he was within. Now in daylight, he realised why the dreamt smell of ginger was such a joy, awake, he could smell nothing. This was probably a relief, vomited raw dog and congealed blood was never marketed as an air freshener plug-in. He wasn't sure he could hear anymore, when he did think he heard things, he didn't trust them.

And what could he do about them anyway?

Was that screaming?

The daylight illuminated a different world now.

There were many more; overnight, the number of carcasses had sharply risen.

Hollow corpses were strewn about. It was as if the minds had given up.

This day was not like any he had ever written about in his diary.

He had found himself openly having sex in the high street. He had been approached, a display was made and within seconds the two of them were rutting by the chain store shoe shop; someone else tried to join in, but they both savaged him. He thought it was Tony, who used to bother people by ringing them to see if they'd thought about having a new kitchen. When the intercourse was finished, he felt unpleasant to have been there. After all, he was now a voyeur. He saw himself as an internet voyeur or someone who rings up a woman on the TV to ask her to shake her bottom more. He had not had a sexual experience, but it had.

He had no trousers now. He concentrated so hard to try and make the muscles and bone reach down and pull back on his clothes, but it ignored him. He presumed that soon, like the others he had seen, he would be naked.

Much of the afternoon was spent punching the window of discount clothes stores. As much as he tried to tell it that this was his own reflection, not some marauding primitive in underpants, it wouldn't listen.

And so he watched what had been his face repeatedly punch and headbutt a plate glass window until it cracked and then shattered. As he looked at that face, the one he had for so many years, the one he had bought cleanser and moisturiser and post-shave balm for, even he wondered if that had really ever been his. He was also embarrassed that it did a victory dance after the reflection was shattered. It had obviously been a good dancer, as he watched itself/himself/whatever having sex again. Annoyingly, it was with Martha, a woman he had always been attracted to but who had married Lucas in error. He should have felt some victory as they howled in unison, but he knew he was not having sex with Martha, she was probably inside her skull wishing that this thing that housed her would stop at once, or at least allow her to put her bra back on. Did she know that it was not him? Would they ever be able to communicate again?

By Thursday, he acknowledged that he wasn't around so much. He presumed it had been staggering around for some hours as he was some way into the countryside when he first felt a smidgen of existence. He noticed the sky moving away from him, this alerted him that he was falling from a branch. Had it been trying to eat acorns or catch a squirrel? It had failed at both.

His awareness seemed to be evaporating, he was that puddle on a hot day, becoming less and less, until it was defined only as a raindrop, and then just the dampness of soil.

He didn't know how many days had passed, but was woken by it beating the water that reflected his face. He had quite a beard. He had never thought a beard would suit him, and he was quite right. He wondered where one of his front teeth had gone.

He hadn't had a dream in a long time. He wondered if empathy and altruism must evolve again or whether these creatures were a last death rattle of sex and violence and solipsism. The babies were left behind and devoured. What banshee cries the mothers within must have tried to unleash as they saw their shell wander away. It was the day he had seen his own signet ring rise to his mouth, a baby's foot in his hand, and then his mouth, that he had resorted to trying to work out if he could kill the self that lay within.

He couldn't watch it anymore. It was too ghastly. All that potential spent.

That stupid frog, was it really a stupid frog, or each time his tongue shot out ninety degrees from the fly he craved, did some inner amphibian cry inside, 'No, you dumb frog tongue, the other way, the other way! Goddamn stupid frog I am.'

MATTHEW HOLNESS

POSSUM

I PICKED IT up by the head, which had grown clammy inside the bag, drawing to it a fair amount of fluff and dirt, and pushed the obscene tongue back into its mouth. Then I blew away the black fibres from its eyes and lifted out the stiff, furry body, attached to its neck with rusted nails. The paws had been retracted by means of a small rotating mechanism contained within the bag handle itself, and I detached the connecting wires from the small circuit pad drilled into its back. Forcing my hand through the hole in its rear, around which in recent months I had positioned a number of small razor blades, I felt within for the concealed wooden handle. Locating it, and ignoring the pain along my forearm, I swerved the head slowly left and right, supporting the main body with my free hand while holding it up against my grubby mirror.

I'd come home to bury it, which was as good a place as any, despite my growing dislike of the mild southern winters. Yet, having stepped from the train carriage earlier that afternoon and sensed, by association I suppose, the stretch of abandoned line passing close behind my old primary school, up towards the beach and the marshes beyond, I'd elected to burn it instead; on one of Christie's stupid bonfires, if he was still up to building them.

Despite my intentions, I'd felt inclined to unveil Possum mid-journey and hold what was left up against the compartment window as we passed through stations; my own head concealed, naturally. But I'd thought better of that; I dare say rightly. In any case, the bag concealing him drew inevitable attention when, entering the underpass on my way back to the house, one of his legs shot out, startling two small boys who were attempting to hurry past. Several adjustments to the internal mechanism in recent years had enabled the puppet's limbs to extend outward at alarming speeds, so that when operated in the presence of suggestible onlookers, it looked as if the legs of some demonic creature, coarse and furred, had darted suddenly from an unseen crevice. Then, as happened rather beautifully on this occasion, the perturbed children, or child, more often than not would catch sight of a second, larger hole, carefully positioned at the rear of the bag to capture their peripheral vision, and glimpse, within, an eye following them home. The effect, I must say, was rather stunning, yet had, like any great performance, taken years to perfect.

Christie had not been at home when I'd arrived, although as usual the front door had been left ajar and the kitchen table crammed with large piles of rubbish awaiting destruction. Stacked among the old comics and clothes I'd found the familiar contents of my bedroom drawer, along with an old tube of my skin cream and a skull fragment I'd once dug up at the beach. Having retrieved these, I'd drunk a large measure of his cheap whisky, tried the lounge door, which, as expected, was locked, then taken my bag up to the bedroom. The walls had been re-papered again with spare rolls from the loft, familiar cartoon faces from either my sixth or seventh year. The boards were still damp, the floor slimy, and a strong odour of paste hung heavily in the cramped room. I'd opened a window – the weather was indeed horribly mild – and switched the overhead bulb off, favouring darkness for what I was about to do.

Although the body was that of a dog, Possum's head was made of wax and shaped like a human's, and I could not have wished for a more convincing likeness. It even captured my old acne scars, yet with hair less neat and a gaunt quality reminiscent of the physical state I had embodied when the mould was made. The eyes were its greatest feature, belonging to what once had been a bull terrier. Both were former lab specimens, heavily diseased, preserved together for years in an old jar of formaldehyde. Several minor adjustments and refinements made by a former colleague, a long-dead teacher of science to whom my work had strangely appealed, had turned them into hard, bright, unique-looking decorations for Possum's face. Deceptively cloudy until caught in the appropriate light, these two vaguely transparent orbs were the key to Possum's success, and, despite patent similarities in our appearance, evidence of his own unique personality.

My most recent addition to his appearance, nevertheless, had also proved extremely effective. At the beginning of summer I had attached coloured flypaper to the tongue, which, like the body, was canine in origin, and over several months the mouth had accrued a large cluster of dead insects that dropped abruptly into view whenever the puppet licked or swallowed, invariably scattering one or two dried bluebottles into my spellbound and horrified audience. This proved to be a striking accessory, particularly as a tiny battery-powered mechanism in the concealed handle allowed me to control rudimentary facial movements, although I had never bothered learning how to throw my voice. Possum's wide-eyed, open-mouthed stare penetrated well enough during his sudden intrusions, without the need of vocal embellishment. Only ever unleashing him at points in my dramas when his presence was a complete surprise, his unnerving silence merely served to exacerbate his chaotic misbehaviour. Whether devouring other characters without warning, usually the hero or heroine, or bursting through walls and destroying with unrestrained violence my neat but tedious endings, Possum's soundless, unpredictable presence captivated my young audiences like no other puppet I'd ever built. He was a law unto himself, and was now even challenging my own authority.

I leaned closer toward the mirror, reflecting on my most recent performance, and watched the sinking sun darken Possum's face with shadow. I observed how his head continued to stir subtly of its own accord as my body's natural rhythms gradually made their way through into his, and I tried in vain to freeze his movements. Before it was fully dark I took Possum outside.

There was no hint of a winter frost, and the earth was suitably wet. I dropped him in the stagnant water tank behind the old shed, where he couldn't get out, and hurled mud and stones down at him from my vantage point at the rim. I pulled faces at him until I could no longer discern anything below, then went back into the house. I considered waiting up for Christie's return, but instead went straight to bed.

I awoke to find Possum beside me, his long tongue hanging out like a vulgar child's. The head had been turned to face me in my sleep, and the eyes in the dawn light were a pale, milky yellow. As I sat up to scratch the tiny bites covering my legs and ankles, several dry house-flies dropped from the pillow onto my bed sheet. Later I found a dead wasp tucked inside my pyjama pocket. I pushed Possum to the floor, noting that his head had been wiped clean and his body scrubbed. Sensing that the parlour games had begun, I dressed quickly. I could hear Christie clattering about in the kitchen below, and I took the puppet with me when I went downstairs.

'Good morning and thank you,' I said, dumping Possum on the table. 'Now please burn all your hard work.'

Christie, moving slowly with the aid of a stick, handed me a mug of strong tea and the ancient cake tin.

'Good morning,' he said, smiling under his thick, nicotine-stained beard. 'The head is expertly made.'

'As are the legs,' I said, sipping my drink. 'A perfect job.'

'*You* wired them in?' he asked.

I looked out at the garden. A huge bonfire had been piled ready.

'I want it burned,' I said. 'That's why I threw it out. You wasted your whole night. Now that's funny.'

Christie laughed, which made me laugh.

'I'm going for a walk,' I added. 'What will you do?'

The old man hobbled slowly across the room, into the hallway.

'I'm going to bed,' he said, and began climbing the

stairs. I waited until he was halfway up, then called out loudly.

'Wasn't your best.'

I interpreted his prolonged silence as a subtle joke and went out into the garden. I inspected Christie's mammoth bonfire, rummaging through the piles of ragged clothes and compost until I located some more of my old possessions buried underneath. I wasn't upset to see my gloves there, but I rescued an old watch my father had given me on my sixth birthday and decided that I would try and mend it. Deep within the piled rubbish was the inevitable roadkill, the largest of which was a mangled fox. I dragged it out by its tail, and as I passed back through the house on my way to the front door, slung it halfway up the stairs, hoping Christie might fall when he bent down to remove it. Then I sealed Possum up in my black bag and walked to the school.

I didn't stop once along the lane, although I saw enough to know that my old classroom, the scene of Christie's infamous stunt, had long since disappeared. An extension to the central building almost blocked my view of the playground, where the brick wall, over which I'd escaped, had been painted over with a large smiling face. I passed the second of two remote mobile classrooms, decorated with tiresome nativity displays, and carried on towards the familiar stone steps leading down to the abandoned station. I followed these onto the empty platform, examining the shelter on the opposite side of the track. Despite an abundance of thick spray-paint and several smashed windows, the place was abandoned. I dropped down silently onto the disused line. The metal tracks had been ripped up long before I was born, and the banks on each side of the route, beyond the declining platform, were heavily overgrown. The ancient trail turned sharply to the left before reaching a small, concealed footpath that snaked off into the trees. I brushed aside overhanging branches as I forced myself along it, pausing several times to pinpoint precisely where I'd once built my secret camp. Further along I located the old tree I'd climbed to impress friends, and the small slope we'd raced down. Beyond these, hidden beneath the thickest trees, was the place I was looking for.

I crouched down on the approaching path and located a suitable vantage point. I made my way over to a dense row of bushes and knelt behind the leaves. The ground around me was littered with empty crisp packets and crushed tins. Nearby lay scattered the feathers of a dead bird. Sooner than I had expected to I developed cramp, and, making as little movement as possible, shifted weight to my hands. Then I settled down to wait, keeping absolutely still.

When the figure finally approached, I opened the bag. Possum's face stared up at me as I drew back the leather, eyes whitening in the overhead sun. I gave him some muddy leaves to eat and was in the process of extricating the rest of his body when I heard movement directly behind. I barely had time to conceal Possum again before a tall man appeared from within the trees. He wore walking shoes and a short winter coat, and carried a school rucksack under one arm. His face was hostile and suspicious.

'Good morning,' I said. Without replying, he moved off swiftly in the direction of the approaching child, calling loudly. I stood up, finding myself unable to move due to the numbness in my legs, and grabbed the handle of my bag. I waited, suspecting that I might require the use of Possum's limbs in order to effect a diversion worthy of pantomime. But no-one else appeared, and the man did not return. As soon as I could, I walked home through a great many winding streets.

'Tell me again about the fox,' Christie said.

'We were in the woods one day and saw a fox. It was panting at the mouth and its whole body was shaking. We thought it had swallowed something bad. When we came back later it was dead. So we played with it a while . . . stuck things in it. Then, as we left for home, the fox stood up. It had been playing with us.'

'I mean the fox you dropped on my stairs,' Christie replied, smugly. Another game won. And putting the dead animal in my bed and laying it out on the kitchen table before me as I ate my breakfast equalled three victories already that morning.

'You shouldn't have stolen from my bonfire,' he said. 'That was misbehaviour.'

I sipped my tea and ate his stale cake. 'Merry Christmas.'

'Not yet, it isn't.'

Christie rose slowly from the table and put on the jacket he'd hung over the back of his chair.

'Not staying?' I said, examining the local paper spread out before me.

'Places to go. The house is your own.'

'I know it is,' I countered. 'And don't you forget it.' One parlour game to me.

'I'll be back at six to start my bonfire.'

I followed him out into the hall, trying the handle of the locked lounge door as I passed, loudly enough for him to hear.

'What happened to our decorations?' I asked. 'We used to have several boxes.'

The old man was struggling with his shoelaces. I didn't help him.

'And what's this with the old caravan site?' I said, indicating the article I'd read.

'Deconstruction,' he replied, eyes focused on his feet.

'It's hideous. What are they putting in its place?'

He stood up, wheezing, and limped forward into mild sunshine.

'Nothing.'

I followed, handing him his walking stick.

'Nothing at all?'

'Not if they find things.' He unearthed a strange-look-ing plant from the ground, exposing a huddle of pink, swollen tubers.

'These shouldn't be ready this time of year.'

I stepped back inside the house.

'I'll have something else for you to burn later. My puppet.'

'Not working any more?' he said, over his shoulder.

'Retired,' I replied, and shut the door on him.

The bleak monotony of the muddy shoreline was lifted only by the distant dance of little red wellingtons far be-hind. Echoes of light laughter overtook me on the breeze as someone closer, concealed on the far side of the ap-proaching breaker, kicked pebbles repeatedly against the wooden barrier. I refrained from operating the bag in this exposed area, progressing instead along the coastal path toward the strange sunken mast that bordered the marsh-es. This tall concrete post stood out bleakly against the horizon, as it had done ever since I was a boy, a rusted

sign nailed to its front stating 'Keep Out'. I was still un-
sure what purpose it had once served, but thought perhaps it could have formed part of an electrical generator
servicing the nearby caravan site. Unchanged, it stood
grim and obsolete while I leaned against it and watched
the trail behind, cradling my cigarette from the wind.

Ahead, the path grew slippery as it rose toward the
crest of a wide ridge overlooking a large, artificial crater.
Formed by a jettisoned wartime bomb, this enclosed ravine was broken only by the slow progress of a shallow,
man-made stream through its centre. The path, dipping
sharply as I continued toward a low wooden bridge,
crossed the green and stagnant water, disappearing again
over the opposite rim.

The bridge itself retained most of its original slats,
yet one or two had fallen away over the years, exposing
a pool of foul silt below. I stepped across, looking down
at the clay bank rising from the water's edge, noticing
several holes in the mud that looked like the work of
small animals. I considered planting Possum inside one
so that my half-buried likeness could surprise the un-
wary children following behind, but then I thought of a
better plan.

Removing Possum from the bag, I left the bridge and
stepped down with him into the stream below, my feet
sinking deep into the thick, oily mud. Using the roll of
tape I always carried with me, I manoeuvred myself beneath the bridge and fastened Possum's body securely
to the rotting planks, directing his face so that the eyes
stared back up through the slats. Returning to the top, I
was pleased to discover that the effect was quite disarm-
ing, and would prove so, I hoped, to my approaching
billy goats.

I left Possum to do his work and moved onward, out of the ravine and across an expanse of wet marsh towards the abandoned caravan site beyond. As I approached, cleansing the mud from my boots in deep puddles, I heard the resounding thud of electrical machinery. The approach to the site involved crossing a stile situated halfway along an elongated hedge, concealing the cabins beyond from view. I was surprised to find, however, that this had now disappeared, along with many of the caravans I had expected to see on the far side. Some distance away, a slow mechanical digger was shifting piles of rubble toward a larger mound. Across what remained of the park stood a few of the oldest cabins, built decades before to capitalise on the town's short-lived tourist trade. Many were blackened by what must have been a recent fire on the site, their walls and doors plastered with offensive graffiti. On one, a small naked doll had been tied to the remains of a twisted television aerial.

As I walked around the edge of the site, away from the digger, I encountered a 'No Trespassing' sign posted up by the local council. Rain began to fall in large, heavy droplets, and the ground rapidly grew sodden. I sat down on an old tyre and watched as the man operating the digger shut off its engine and wandered over to a small truck parked at the far edge of the site. The vehicle moved off onto the main road and headed back towards town, leaving the site deserted.

I felt around in my bag for my tool case. Opening it, I removed a small chisel I kept with me for repairs and began to sift through the mud around my feet, smelling the yellow earth caught on its metal blade. I carved a large smiling face into the muddy ground and watched as the rain slowly destroyed its features, then walked back to collect Possum.

At first I thought the tape must have worked loose in the rain, but then I saw how far the puppet had moved from the vicinity of the bridge, and decided that a real dog must have dragged it there. It couldn't have been one of the children, and closer examination of the muddy bank behind Possum revealed small paw marks, almost completely eroded by the recent downfall. Possum's head had been mauled at the ears, and one of the eyes was protruding slightly more prominently than usual. I kicked him around in the wet for a while and stamped hard on his face, wondering whether it was worth burying him permanently beneath the mud at the caravan site. Then I remembered the digger, packed him up in my bag and walked home.

'I'd like a demonstration before I burn him,' said Christie, opening two tins of cheap lager for us. 'Nothing special, but I want to see how the legs work.'

'Trade secret,' I replied, lighting the candles. When this was done he finally removed our meals from the oven.

'What other puppets do you use?'

'Several, but I want this one burned.'

He served me the larger dish, which I realised was the dead fox.

'I heard about your last performance,' he said, popping his half-smoked cigarette in Possum's mouth, whom I'd sat in the guest's chair between us. 'One of my old teaching colleagues wrote to me about it. An unpredictable affair, by all accounts.'

I ignored the comment and jabbed at the sticky burnt carcass staring up at me from my plate.

'I don't like this,' I said. 'Care to swap?'

Grinning, my host tucked greedily into what appeared to be a small bird.

'You forgot party crackers,' I said, sipping from my tin.

'And grace,' he replied, removing a small shred of bone from his upper lip.

'They'll take me back,' I said, poking my fork at Possum, 'once *he's* gone.'

'We'll need gloves to get rid of it,' Christie said. 'It's diseased.'

I examined my hands, which I sensed were peeling terribly and starting to bleed, and felt my face. I was covered.

'Eczema,' I said, hiding what I could of me beneath the table.

'Remember,' said Christie, his mouth full. 'A demonstration.'

The front half of the cabin was severely smoke-damaged, although in places I could still make out graffiti beneath the blackened panelling. The place stank of urine and petrol, and I sat at the back with my bag, near to where the bathroom had once been, and watched the remains of the site through a charred breach in the van opposite.

It was about midday when I crouched down on my knees so that I could not see out and crawled across the cabin floor. I examined where the cupboard used to be and touched the far side of the rear wall with my hands, feeling for the faint words scratched somewhere upon its surface. I leaned closer, sniffing at the floor, then gasped suddenly and withdrew. I stood up, returned to the seat, and opened my black bag.

I pulled Possum out and sat him on my lap. His body felt softer on one side. When I pressed my fingers against the fur, the insides gave a little, and I assumed they must be damaged in some way. His protruding eye, too, had broken open. A crack to the outer shell had caused a small leakage that ran down Possum's face, looking like dried egg yolk and smelling vaguely of chemicals.

I pulled his tongue down and tucked stray hairs behind his mauled ears. The wiring mechanism now broken, I extended, manually, each of his legs, until he sat astride me. I lay back against the seat, stretching my body lengthways, pulling him on top of me so that his face rested inches from my own. I slung his two front paws over my shoulders, opened my own mouth to mirror his, and stared back into his contaminated eyes. Then, with my tongue, I removed one of the dead flies from his.

'Don't,' I said, and swallowed it. One by one, I ate them all. When Possum's mouth was clear, I lifted him from me, very gently, and sat myself up. I resisted the urge to retch and removed the tool case from my black bag. Having selected a blade, I picked up Possum, bit his ear without warning and threw him roughly to the floor. I knelt down on top of him and sawed at his nose, slowly and methodically, until I had sliced off its tip. I stuffed the severed segment inside his mouth and angled his limbs against the floor. With my boot I snapped each joint in turn and threw the broken legs out of the open window. I seized Possum's torso and thrust my arm inside. Crying out as the razors cut deeply into my wounds, I smashed the puppet hard against the wall, rocking the unstable cabin, before scraping the mutilated face against every sharp and jagged surface I could see. I removed my arm then, which was bleeding heavily, and took the scissors from my tool bag. I snipped off Possum's hair and jammed the tattered clumps between his teeth. I stabbed his eyes repeatedly with both blades until the weak one gave way entirely, spurting a glob of liquid over my fingers and up the scissor blade. I spat back at him, attempting to gouge a channel from one eyehole to the other, across his nose. The wax proved too strong, and instead I cut my own fingers. Grabbing a blunt wooden pole from my bag, I struck his head several times before shoving the blunt end of the pole into his mouth. When I'd finished thrusting, his head pinned and useless against the cabin wall, I gathered what was left of him beneath my arm and threw him into the corner. I kicked his stomach repeatedly until it caved in, exposing the stained wooden handle inside. I stuffed the belly with junk and threw Possum through the broken doorway, out into the yard beyond. Then I sucked the blood from my fingers, picked up my bag and left the cabin.

I stood as close to the flames as I could bear, hoping that my clothes would retain the smell of smoke. Christie shovelled in another heap of rubbish, momentarily stifling the blaze. I opened my bag and pulled out Possum's head, which I'd severed from his body with a spade while Christie had ransacked the last of my bedroom cupboards.

'Season's greetings,' I said, tossing it across the grass towards him. 'Too late for a demonstration.'

'You should let me fix it,' he said. 'I like fixing things.'

I lifted up the headless remains and threw them

on the bonfire. Smoke curled around the bent, twisted nails wrenched incompletely from the neck as a sharp, sulphurous odour burned my nostrils. Flames snapped loudly against the coarse, brown fur as Christie held up the decapitated head and laughed.

'A broken toy,' he said. 'You shouldn't have.'

'I saw it and thought of you,' I replied, which made him laugh even more. I lit us both cigarettes while Christie perched what remained of Possum on an old wooden stool. He stuck his own inside the puppet's mouth and begged another. When we'd finished, he lifted up the head ceremoniously and dropped it on the bonfire, along with my watch, smiling to himself as he jammed them deep into the blazing compost with his pitchfork.

'How will you spend your Christmas day?' he asked.

'Exercising,' I replied.

'Exorcising?'

'Past the school, if you must know.'

'The school.' Christie's face was a mischievous grin. 'I taught you there once.'

'I know. You died reading us a story.'

'I came especially, the day after that business with the fox. To teach you all a lesson.'

I watched Possum's face blacken and bubble, collapsing gradually into soft clear rivers of molten wax.

'Now that was a game to remember,' Christie continued. 'The looks on your faces. You should have seen yourselves.'

'I'll be out all day,' I said, zipping up my coat.

'Children talk such rot.' The flames began to rise again as he turned over a pile of burning rags. 'When there's no one there to reassure them.'

The eyes fell out together, exposing two pallid-looking sockets. I went inside and tried, without success, to force open the lounge door.

I had meant to purchase my return ticket, but realised upon reaching the station that there would be no trains leaving until the following day. I wandered for an hour or so until I gathered enough courage to enter one of the few pubs that were open. There I stomached a strong whisky and some fatty sandwiches as the sun went down, before heading out once more, away from insufferable partygoers, into the darkness of the surrounding streets.

I gazed into people's houses through open blinds as I passed. The gaudy house-fronts, plastered with coloured lights and cheap decorations, one after another, left me feeling lost, so I sought darker avenues as I fled the town centre in the direction of my old school.

The ground through the adjacent lane was slippery, as if many people had been rushing along it during the day, and I found myself slowing involuntarily and glancing across at the disparate group of buildings that made up the school. A single lamp lit the area of the playground, exposing the large painted face that marked the area where Christie had chased us, full of life, having feigned his terrifying heart attack. Someone, I assumed a janitor, was watching television in a small hut on the far side of the concrete field. I stopped for a moment to stare at the small alley in which I had sat alone many times during that final year, attempting to make sense of all that had happened to me. When I heard something enter the lane behind me, I moved on, quickening my pace.

I raced down the stone steps, crossed the old platform and dropped down onto the abandoned line, pausing only to adjust my vision once more to the surrounding darkness. I moved off carefully, the noise of my footfalls interrupted only by the soft rush of wind moving through the nearby treetops. It took me longer than usual, but I eventually found the small hidden pathway into the trees and walked along it, noting that the ground here, like the school lane, was wetter and more broken up than before.

I found the place again instinctively, clear as the event still was in my memory, and stood up straight upon the spot, making sure I didn't slouch or bend my back in any way. I unzipped my coat and drew out the small lunch box I'd filled secretly after Christie had left the house. I removed the lid and, one by one, thrust my peeling hands into Possum's ashes, noting the sharp, unpleasant smell my skin now emitted. Once I was satisfied that the remains were truly soiled, I tipped the powdered mess onto the ground where the man had first shown himself to me, and smeared what was left into the earth, tossing the empty box into a nearby bush, near where he'd dragged me.

It was while I was wiping my hands clean with my handkerchief that I heard the dog. It had followed me through the empty station and was nosing through the bushes behind, tracking my scent. I thought of playing dead, but then strode out onto the footpath, holding out my diseased hands that he'd hated touching. I screamed loudly at the top of my voice and this time the dirty creature stalking me ran a mile.

I mouthed words into the telephone receiver as my fingers tapped nervously on the dull, metallic surface of the rotary dial, flashing blue lights from the distant caravan site reflected against it. When I looked up again, the policeman who'd walked over to watch me hadn't moved.

'He put me in his bag,' I said aloud, to the faint, hypnotic hum of the dial tone. 'Then he carried me to his caravan.'

The rain had returned. I peered out across the grass slope, trying to look preoccupied, as the policeman made his decision and moved toward me.

'He always covered his face,' I said, suddenly desperate for air. I nudged the door ajar.

'. . . he never took it off.'

I hung up. Foolishly, as the officer reached me, I smiled.

'On your way,' he ordered, studying my features. As I walked back to town, one of their cars followed me home.

Christie was drunk when he opened the door, and laughed openly at the state of my hands.

'That won't help you.'

I snatched the bottle from him and wandered through into the kitchen, swigging heavily from it. The linoleum floor stuck to the soles of my shoes.

'I'm leaving tomorrow,' I said.

'Are you?' he replied.

'Thanks for putting me up.'

'Always a pleasure.' He grinned inanely, performing an awkward, drunken dance. 'Always was.'

He began to sing an obscene song.

'Why don't you go to bed?' I snapped, taking another swig from the bottle. Swaying, I leant down and put what was left back in the cupboard under the sink.

'Your present's in the lounge,' he said.

I lost balance, then, and dropped to the floor. My hands touched dirt as I crawled towards the corner of the room.

'Sorry everything's so late.' He stopped moving long enough to light a cigarette. He seemed younger to me. 'I'll have a car collect you tomorrow.'

'They've found something up at the site,' I said, eventually.

Christie inhaled deeply, knelt down and blew his smoke in my face.

'They have indeed.'

Suddenly sheepish, he giggled pathetically, stood and stumbled off in the direction of the stairs, moving up them much faster than I'd thought he was capable of.

I didn't go in there immediately, as the whisky had made me feel nauseous. I smoked a couple more cigarettes and listened for a while to Christie breaking my things in the room above.

When I did finally enter our lounge, unlocked for the first time in decades, I saw that nothing had changed since the day Christie first appeared with news of my bereavement. The tree was still there, its branches bare since the night of their funeral when he'd got me drunk for the first time and burned our decorations in front of me. I looked up to the top, where my Daddy had once lifted me to place our fairy, and saw something else I recognised.

It was the man's dog mask, and although now I could see only the wall behind through its cruel eyeholes, I realised it had belonged to Christie after all, and he'd worn it here beside me all these years, waiting for my courage to awaken.

Below, beneath the tree, was my present, wrapped up

in newspaper and tied at the top with an ancient ribbon. It was a large, odd-looking object, bearing an old gift tag addressed to me that hung, quite still, from a small thread of dull, red cotton.

As I crawled toward the parcel, it twitched suddenly and a faint rustling sounded from the wrapping where the taut sheets began to bulge rapidly back and forth, as though something trapped beneath them were trying to breathe. When its long leg burst through the paper and pawed violently at the carpet in front, teeming with life, I reached out eagerly to unwrap my Possum.

KATY BRAND

FOR ROGER

ROGER WAS WOKEN by the sound of scrabbling from within the walls. He had woken to the sound several times this summer, but it had never been loud enough to be the cause of his waking before. He lay in bed for a few moments, just listening, allowing his other senses to come into play. It sounded like rodents – if you have one mouse, you have a thousand – he'd heard that somewhere, a long time ago. Was it a singular mouse, trapped in the wall? Or a family in a nest, made from insulation and bits of whatever else mice feel safe in? Did the scrabbler mean to be there? Or had it accidentally become encased in a brick tomb? If Roger did nothing, would the scrabbler die, or multiply? Hard to say; he got up.

Downstairs, Roger's wife was already in the kitchen, drinking tea and reading the local paper.

'I think there's a mouse in the wall,' Roger said as he reboiled the kettle.

'If you've got one mouse, you've got a thousand,' Roger's wife said, without looking up. 'There's a story here about the new housing development up near the burnt-out barn. People getting very het up about it.'

Roger didn't care about the new housing development – the burnt-out barn was over two miles away, and in any case he thought a new influx of families would be good for the village, which was already stagnating in the still waters of an ageing population living in houses with perfectly preserved but entirely empty bedrooms, sentimentally held for children long since gone. But the local community feared for the value of their properties, believing that any new houses would damage the upward trend they had all enjoyed for decades. They all intended to leave their Georgian and Victorian cottages to their children, and their children all intended to sell them immediately in order to cover the inheritance tax and their own outstanding debts. Who would buy the houses was not immediately apparent as no young family could afford the market value and the rich pensioners would all be dead, but that was not part of the conversation anyone on the Parish Council was willing to have.

'Should I make a hole in the plasterboard and see what's in there?' Roger asked.

'Best call the pest controller, I'd say. Or just leave them to it – they're not doing any harm, are they?'

'They woke me up this morning.'

'Well, you should be getting up anyway – it's nearly nine, and you don't want to sleep the day away.' Roger's wife rose, rinsed her cup and kissed him. 'I'd best be off – I'll see you later. What have you got planned? Anything?'

Roger shrugged, though not unhappily; these long, empty days were still a novelty following his recent retirement as a maths teacher from the local FE college. He could feel boredom and futility flickering around the edges, but he would find a hobby before they really took hold. For now, he was happy just pottering. Roger's wife was a few years younger and still worked at the library, although with closures all over the county, redundancy was always in the air. She didn't mind too much – their pensions would see them comfortably through – perhaps the last generation who could say that with any certainty, and though hers would not come into force for a while yet, Roger's generous teacher's pension scheme, just nipped in time before the major changes were imposed, would keep them until then.

Roger watched his wife walk through the living room and on to the front door. She had a big bottom, he observed for the millionth time, but not flabby. It was firm and high and jostled nicely within her trousers. She didn't like it, but Roger was always quick to reassure her. 'Men like a bottom they can park their bike in and rest their pint on,' he would say, and she would giggle and feel better.

Roger took his tea and toast into the garden and stood facing the house. He looked up at the bedroom, as if he might somehow be able to learn more about the scrabbler from its exterior. He allowed his eyes to roam over the old red brick, inlaid with relatively freshly painted white wooden window frames and discreetly double glazed panes that kept at bay the noise of the A road which lay just beyond an attractive line of trees to the west. He looked up, beyond the bedroom window, to the gabled roof under which was a loft space they had considered converting but never bothered once it was clear that they would be a one-child family. The chimney above was both pretty and functional, and provided, Roger thought, an ideal access point for all sorts of wildlife during the summer months. This he knew because last year, while he and his wife were watching a documentary about the multiverse theory of existence on BBC4, a raven had landed startled and startling in the fireplace, closely followed by clumps of twig and feather that had been the beginnings of a nest. It had badly broken its wing in the fall and Roger had killed it with a brick and buried it in the wood – a curiously sentimental thing for him to do, but they had both felt that putting it in the bin was somehow disrespectful or barbaric, or something else unnamed but uncharacteristically pagan in nature.

Roger drained his cup and went inside. He changed out of his pyjamas and put on his pottering about clothes – an old pair of chinos and a light cotton shirt with a button missing. He went into the spare room-cum-study, pulled the pole with the brass hook on the end from its usual place in the corner behind the bookshelf and held it up to the wooden hatch door in the ceiling. Sliding the hook into the catch he pulled it open and unhinged the folding ladder that lay in the space above. He made sure the base was hard pressed against the floor and the safety catch fully clicked in place at the top, leant the pole against the wall and climbed into the loft. Flicking the switch screwed into a wooden rafter at the top of the ladder, the space was now gently bathed in the weak light emanating from a single, uncovered bulb at waist height in another rafter.

The loft was amateurishly boarded, work undertaken by the previous owner in order to advertise a 'boarded loft' when he put it on the market, and was just robust enough to take the weight of an average man and a few storage boxes, sleeping bags and black sacks with stickers saying things like 'spare duvet' on them. Roger could stand to his full height in the centre of the loft but had to stoop as he moved to the side, and then finally drop to his knees as the roof met the floor around the square edges. The cold water tank stood quiet, black and monolithic in one corner.

Roger stood still in the centre of the loft and strained his ears. There was a low hum – pipework, plumbing and such – but yes, there it was: the scrabbling. He could see the outline of the brick chimney breast on the east wall and this was directly above the bedroom he shared with his wife, which in turn was directly above the living room. In fact, their bedroom still had an old Victorian fireplace in it, long since bricked up and not used for over five decades. When Roger and his wife had bought the house twenty-three years ago they had considered unblocking it but never got round to it. Perhaps they would now Roger was retired – it was a dream of his since childhood to warm his feet at the end of his bed by the glow of burning coals. Roger moved towards the chimney breast, stooping as he went, seeming to rewind evolution with his posture until he crawled on all fours to the base of the brick flue. He pressed his ear against the floor and once again the scrabbling could be heard. Sitting back on his haunches, Roger was able to lift the loose board he had been kneeling on and put it to one side. Pulling his cuffs over his hands, he gently rolled back the fibre glass insulation underneath. Another layer of ply was underneath that which would not take even a child's weight, but where it was supposed to meet the wall there was a gap of around two inches by eight. That'll be where the little buggers have got in, Roger thought, and noted a collection of small droppings around the sides. He gingerly slid his finger into the gap, thinking all the while that this was a bad idea, that mice could bite, especially a mouse guarding its young, or trapped and frightened, and hooked it under the ply segment. It was loose, as if it had been pulled up before, and though it would not lift out entirely, it moved to create a gap large enough for Roger to put his whole hand into the space beneath. He had no idea what he would find – the interior workings of a house were as much a mystery to him as the social lives of some of his former A-level students, but he was absorbed now and curiosity led him on like a golden thread.

Reaching down into the space, his arm was buried up to the elbow. He felt around blindly and then his fingers brushed something unexpected. It was the hard edge of what could be a small book. It had a rough cover and as Roger's fingers explored its proportions, his mind created the image of a diary or notebook of the kind he often used to make notes in the classroom in order to keep track of pupils' progress or lesson plans. He took the book in his grip and twisted it back through the gap. It was as he expected: it was exactly like the notebooks he had always used – a black, rough, hard-backed cover with ruled pages inside. It was even the same brand; he would buy them in bulk every August and put them aside at the end of each academic year. He could never quite bring himself to throw them away and most of them were packed into the very boxes that now surrounded him. How on earth had this one managed to get itself under here? Roger sat back, wiped the dust off the cover and opened it.

Printed on the first page in his own handwriting formed in ink from his own familiar fountain pen were the words, 'For Roger'. He frowned – he had no recollection of writing this; he had never begun a notebook like this before – his usual formulation was simply his full name, the date and the address of the college, should the book in question ever go astray. But 'For Roger' . . . 'For Roger' made no sense. And yet Roger's heart was pounding because there was no doubt that it was he who had written those two words; he had a distinctive hand, looping and formal, carried proudly through his life from a formative period at a German school before he was ten years old, where the dying art of proper handwriting was, and still is, prized. He smoothed the palm of his hand over the page as if trying to absorb some explanatory vibration, but all this was just procrastination from what was clearly the next logical step: page two.

Roger breathed in quickly through his nose and turned the page. His disbelief could not overcome the reality as he read, again in his own hand, the message neatly laid out there:

Dear Roger,

Now that you have found this, I can't say whether life will get easier or harder – it is what it is. Please accept my very best wishes for your future.

From Roger

Sitting down in the semi-darkness of the loft, surrounded by quiet, uncomplaining items from his life that had proved themselves unnecessary, Roger tried to keep hold of some kind of sense of his reality. The scrabbling may or may not have stopped, but it didn't matter, because the listener was now effectively deaf to anything other than the buzzing in his ears. What he was holding in his hands could not be what it appeared to be and therefore, he thought, it must be something else. Page three beckoned. And there, Roger read with widening eyes and thumping pulse:

July 13th: *Went into loft to investigate possible mouse in the wall. Found a book under the floorboards that appears to be from myself. Not sure what on earth to do with it.*

Yes, he thought to himself, yes, today is July 13th. Yes, that is the date, that is the date today, that is today's date. He snapped the book shut and threw it across the loft. It hit the water tank and landed fatly on the board beneath. Roger was breathing fast now, fast enough to hyperventilate if he didn't stop. He took several deep breaths, thinking of a story in the local paper some years back about a man who had lain dead and undiscovered in his loft for over a year. Of course, that wouldn't happen to Roger – the ladder was down for a start, indicating his whereabouts, and his wife would be home around four and would find his body in no time. But regardless of all that, he didn't want to die, not now. He felt out of control, something he hated more than anything. He didn't know why he had thrown the book, he was not a man given to throwing things other than cricket balls on a Sunday afternoon at the local club. It was most out of character. He sat, calming himself using a relaxation technique he had learnt at a meditation seminar on a cruise, and regarded the silent book as if it were a large spider he had not yet configured a plan to get rid of. He wondered if, like a spider, it might just go away of its own accord if he descended the loft ladder, shut the hatch and forgot about it. Or would he, as in a nightmare, awake in the middle of the night to find it crawling into his mouth, long, jointed legs probing his throat as it did so.

Roger crawled over to the book and then stood up so that he towered over it. He prodded it a little with his toe, nudging it an inch or two along the board. He wondered whether it would disintegrate in his hands if he picked it up and tried to take it downstairs. Strange things happened in lofts – Roger had seen enough films to know that – they had their own spellbound reality. If you took something like this out of its environment and down into the land of the living, perhaps a rational explanation would present itself. Yes, he would do that, he would disempower this thing by pulling it into normal space/time, that is to say, the kitchen. Nothing eerie ever happens in kitchens, Roger thought to himself, people have cups of tea and explain things in kitchens, so that's where I will go.

He grabbed the book and climbed down the ladder, then down the stairs and then fast through the living room and into the place where the kettle lived and therefore order. He put the book down on the table, covered in its bright, floral plastic cloth, and set the water to boil for another cup of tea. A thousand identical books had sat in its place over the years, full of notes on teaching quadratic equations and polynomials and De Moivre's Theorem. As Roger watched his teabag bob gently in the hot water, the liquid becoming darker, murkier, he willed the thing sitting not five feet away from him now to transform into one of these benign books of numbers and well-meant scribblings. He added milk and went to sit with it. After three sips he opened the front cover again. 'For Roger', it said. He shut it and looked out of the kitchen window. A blue tit bobbed onto the bird feeder, grabbed a seed and bobbed off again. A moment later, an identical blue tit bobbed on and bobbed off again. You would have to be an expert to tell them apart, Roger mused, or perhaps they were the same bird.

Roger suddenly felt better. He was being silly, he thought. He must have written this as some sort of joke years ago and hidden it. Or perhaps his son, when still a teenager, perfectly mimicked his handwriting and then forgotten about it. That doesn't explain the date though and that the entry for that date perfectly matches what you have done today, was his follow-up thought. Co-incidence, thought Roger the maths teacher, it can be explained. The probability is small, but still, it can be explained. He rested his hand on the top of the book as if to control it. He would call his son later and ask him all about it, and his son would remember and laugh at the childish prank that took ten years to come to fruition. Why not call him now? Roger didn't know why he resisted that course of action, but something stopped him. Did he want to believe there was something more to the book, in spite of himself? A shaft of sunlight beamed through the French windows and with it came enough of a sense of safety for Roger to open the book and turn to the next entry.

July 14th: *Spent most of the day wondering whether to show Rosemary the book or whether it will upset her too much. Don't know whether I am too upset to look at it again myself.*

And now Roger felt the creeping dread, because all

of a sudden he understood that the rest of the book was bubbling beneath his fingertips. The rest of the book. Or rather, the rest of his life. And now he was compelled to look, compelled to do the very thing that no reader wants to do but sometimes cannot help. He turned to the back page.

December 14th: *Went for a walk, just to get out of the house. James is coming home for Christmas, which will be nice. I could certainly use the company.*

And then, nothing. That was the last entry. After that, blank page after blank page. What did it mean? Why was there nothing more? He knew though, deep inside, he knew. And why could he 'use the company'? He knew that too, and flicked back until he found it.

September 9th: *Rosemary died today. I don't know what to do. It's too much of a shock.*

Roger stared at that page for a very long time. His tea went cold. September 9th – eight weeks away by a rough calculation. How? How had she died? Would it tell him? Did he want to know? Could it be prevented? He read frantically through the pages preceding September 9th, but there was nothing – just banal thoughts on the state of the garden and the latest Parish Council vote on the housing development – Christ, was his life really this boring? Some thoughts here and there on the beauty of Rosemary's smile made him pause, as did the odd account of a romantic dinner at an expensive restaurant, and most arresting of all, the resumption of their sex life. Chastely put of course, with no details, but it was certainly something which had been absent for some years.

That was surprising. But nothing, nothing on the cause of death – no hint of any medical issues that could have led up to it. It must have been an accident, an awful, horrifying accident.

Roger turned to the pages following September 9th, desperate for some clue – there was nothing at all for the week after, presumably while he got over the shock, and then just sparse notes on the doctors being very helpful and some brief information about the funeral ('Rosemary's Aunt Doris came, which was a huge surprise'). He cursed himself for his lack of creative ability when it came to writing – why hadn't he elaborated on the detail? Why hadn't he indulged in long descriptive passages about his feelings, or the exact nature of what had happened? Why was he so closed up all the time, just as Rosemary and James had often said in accusatory tones? He shut the book hard in defiance and walked away from it. He didn't have to believe it, he thought. And in any case, there was too much about it that made no sense. Why did it only start today, the day he had happened to find it? What if he had found it yesterday? Would it have begun then instead? Or tomorrow? And if so, would the following entries all be different? Would Rosemary live past September 9th, and he past December 14th? And now he caught himself, because he was taking the book seriously and that was crazy. Yes, that was craziness, to believe that this book really was telling the future, or the past, or whatever it was. He wasn't writing it now, was he, so who had? Who had written the book? Which 'Roger' was this, who had recorded every day and left it in the loft the day before he apparently died, or for some reason had stopped making entries? Was it a different Roger? Had another Roger lived in this house at some point in history, and by some incredible coincidence also had a wife named Rosemary and a son named James, and had also ventured into the loft to look for a mouse on July 13th? Roger noted that there was no year given in the book, so it could have happened anytime in the past. Or the future – yes, maybe he was not the intended recipient of the book,– perhaps it was meant for a different, future Roger, and not him at all. Roger looked around, bewildered. He was at the end of the garden though he had no recollection of walking there. He could see the whole of his house from here: the kitchen, the bedroom window, the gabled roof, the chimney. He wished he had never gone up there. He cursed the mouse, or mice, or whatever it was, that had led him there in the first place.

He would burn the book, he decided. And then pretend he had never seen it. If it didn't exist then it couldn't harm him. Or Rosemary, or anyone named Roger who happened to chance upon it. But no – perhaps that was a mistake. Burning it could increase its potency, he thought wildly, like a sacrifice, or offering. No, the best thing he could do would be to return it to its hiding place, roll back the insulation, replace the top board, turn off the light, exit the loft, push the ladder up and click the panel back into the hatch and forget about it. Just forget about it. As if he had never discovered it. Yes, that was the best thing he could do. And that is exactly what he did.

A couple of hours later, Rosemary arrived home to find the house pristine and Roger waiting for her with a chilled bottle of Chablis to enjoy together in the garden. He was touched by her obvious delight and cursed himself for not having treated her like this more often. As she chatted about her day he longed to tell her about the book, to see her laugh incredulously, to find some explanation for the horror it held, and then to tease him gently for having got so wound up about it. But he couldn't, he couldn't find the words, he couldn't even start the sentence. 'Rosemary, I found a book in the loft that seems to be from some other version of me and it says you will die unexpectedly on September 9th this year. I don't know what it is or where it has come from, but it seemed to know what I was doing today, and I can also see already that it has summed up tomorrow fairly accurately, too.' It occurred to him, as Rosemary poured herself a second glass and turned her face up to the late afternoon summer sun, that by telling her about the book he would in fact render the entry for July 14th inaccurate, thereby possibly disempowering it altogether, but even then he could not get the words out. He felt that by saying them out loud they might become true, which was a symptom of OCD. He knew this because his father had suffered acutely from that condition, but Roger had always assumed he had not inherited it.

And besides, Rosemary was on the move now, thinking about preparing dinner. She limped ever so slightly into the kitchen and Roger wondered whether that was significant. He followed her in.

'Why are you limping?'

'Oh, I don't know, I think I strained a calf muscle at Pilates last night and it doesn't seem to want to heal. Getting old, see?' She smiled at him warmly, full of the promise of their retirement together.

'Perhaps you shouldn't go to Pilates anymore,' said Roger helplessly.

'Oh, don't be silly – it's good for me. It's only a little ache.' Roger nodded, enclosed in his own silent hell and went back outside as Rosemary happily, tipsily pulled pans out of the cupboard and found an onion to slice.

As the summer days passed, Roger and Rosemary had never appeared happier. Roger continued to surprise Rosemary with little gifts and tokens: evenings out, open-air jazz nights, wine tastings, expensive meals, a weekend in a posh hotel where finally the sexual drought that had hung around both their necks for the best part of five years was broken, and many more tiny moments that made their marriage live again. She had never looked more beautiful to him and he told her often. He even persuaded her to go part time at the library and on the days she did work, he would bring a hamper full of wonderful, luxury food and drink to share in the park nearby. He was careful to keep busy during the days she wasn't around, volunteering with the Parish Council to help clear paths and the pond, and even attending the odd meeting if Rosemary was at her Pilates class – anything to get him out of the house. He wished August could last forever. He wished September would never come.

But come it did, and Roger felt the first of the month like a stone in his stomach. He lay in bed as Rosemary slept beside him, staring up at the ceiling, the book lying there above him, only a few feet of air and an inch or two of plasterboard between them. It couldn't be true, he told himself. It couldn't be true, because it was a mathematical impossibility. And then the thousands of theories that had fascinated him as a student, that had whispered that all kinds of things were possible in purely mathematical terms, that we know only a fraction of what the true nature of mathematical reality could hold, would reach their long bony fingers into his mind until he wanted to cry out and hold Rosemary's warm, solid, snoring body tight and never let go.

The first of the month turned to the second, the second to the third, and it was all Roger could do to keep the rising panic at bay. Rosemary asked him several times what was wrong, proving that despite his best efforts he was not concealing it as well as he'd hoped to. He couldn't tell her, he couldn't. 'In five days you will die, darling. In four . . . in three . . . in two . . . tomorrow.' His eyes felt hollow and sunken, and as the nights became noticeably longer, Rosemary voiced her concern. Over dinner, on the 8th of September she said, 'I think you should see a doctor.' Roger stifled a laugh, a bitter, mirthless laugh, and merely nodded. He took her hand and looked her square in the face.

'Will you stay at home with me from midnight tonight to midnight tomorrow?' Rosemary was bemused at the seriousness of his tone.

'I have work . . .'

'Can you call in sick?'

'Well, Maria's just had a baby, so we're short-staffed . . .'

'Please. Please do this for me. Please. I will explain after midnight tomorrow, if . . . if possible.' Rosemary cocked her head. She knew of Roger's father's mental health issues towards the end of this life, and had often wondered if the same ghosts would ever come to haunt her husband.

'OK, darling, OK – if that's what you need, I can . . . this once. And then, maybe see the doctor?'

'Yes, of course.'

They finished their meal quietly and went to bed early.

Rosemary fell asleep, but Roger had no intention of letting his guard down. As the clock flipped itself to 00.00 on the bedside table, he lay facing his wife and listened carefully for every breath. He lay like this all night and his eyelids did not droop once. When Rosemary stirred around seven, as was her habit, he sat up with her at once. He followed her to the bathroom and waited outside while she relieved herself. He went with her down the stairs and stood with her while she made tea and then drank it with her at the table. He pushed the bathroom door slightly ajar while she bathed and then hovered in the bedroom while she dressed. He suggested they spend the day indoors, reading quietly together, or listening to music, and she, with some concern for her husband, agreed. They ate lunch together in the kitchen and Roger was careful to prepare a meal that contained absolutely no choking hazards. After lunch they sat in the living room and read passages from favourite books to one another. Rosemary was wary of her husband and had made a mental note to call the doctor the following morning, whether he liked it or not. Perhaps retirement was affecting him after all. Roger watched the clocks – as the hours ticked by and no sign of anything untoward presented itself, he started to wonder if he was indeed going a little mad. He could tell Rosemary was concerned, but felt it was worth it – if he could just get her to midnight alive, the book would be wrong and all would be well. By four o'clock he was exhausted and he let his head tip back on the couch as Rosemary sat opposite and read from *David Copperfield*. Her voice was soft and soothing and Roger let his eyelids droop and close. Soon he was drifting away on a ribbon of sleep.

When he awoke, the room felt cold. He started up

from the sofa, furious with himself for letting his concentration slip. Rosemary was dead in her chair. Roger sat up straight and stared at her lifeless face. The book was still in her hands. 'Cup of tea, love?' he said to himself, for there was now no one else in the room. He crept over to where she sat and knelt at her feet. He wrapped his arms around her knees and whispered, 'I'm sorry, I'm sorry.'

When Roger called an ambulance an hour or so later he accompanied his wife to the hospital, where he was informed that she had died suddenly and probably without pain from a massive thrombosis moving from her calf to her heart. They asked Roger if she had had any pain in her leg in the months leading up to her death and Roger confirmed that she had. They asked if he had anyone at home to keep him company and Roger confirmed that his son James was coming to help. And then he collapsed, right there in the hospital, and was there for a week before he regained consciousness and was told he had had a moderately sized stroke. He was kept in for a few more days and then sent home, where James was already in situ, ready to take care of his father.

Roger's recovery was slow, but James could take the time – he ran his own business and could effectively work from anywhere and he had an understanding girlfriend who came and went as her own job allowed. Roger was grateful and ashamed, and as he lay in bed and the weeks passed, all he could think of was the book, the book, the book. Why didn't it contain any useful information about Rosemary's death? Why hadn't he written to himself that he should pay attention to the calf injury? He had been so consumed with her impending demise that he had not noticed the signs that could have protected her from it and he cursed himself. He took his medicine, and did his physio, and got stronger, but still the book plagued him. He began to look forward to the 14th of December, supposedly his last on earth, and wished that he could get into the loft to read every entry between now and then so he could follow it to the letter and be sure to bring about his own passing.

By late November, Roger could walk with relative confidence and prepare food and wash himself and he was keen to get James out of the house and back to his own life. Too much of your time has been wasted here, he told his son, and was deaf to protest. And so finally, James went back to his flat with the promise to visit at the weekend. Roger walked a little every day, thinking only of the book and December 14th. He wished he could speed up time, he wished the day would come sooner – every hour was a tortuous, slow grope through a twilight reality. He no longer belonged here. Until finally, it came. He could remember the entry for that day exactly:

December 14th: *Went for a walk, just to get out of the house. James is coming home for Christmas, which will be nice. I could certainly use the company.*

Roger awoke early, made himself tea and toast and sat in the living room with the phone beside him until it rang.

'Hello James,' he said upon picking it up.

'Oh, hi Dad, how are you feeling?'

'I'm well, son, how are you?'

'I'm good – so, look, I've cancelled the holiday, so I can come to you for Christmas, but is it OK if I bring Polly?'

Roger nodded to himself – yes, this was how it should go.

'Of course. I could certainly use the company.' He permitted himself a wry smile.

'OK great – take care and we'll see you on the 24th, OK? Can you manage 'til then?'

'No problem.'

Roger rang off and stood. He gathered his things together for the walk he would now go on, just to get out of the house.

The day was high and bright, the sky blue and fresh, cold but not unbearable. It brought a touch of rose to Roger's cheeks. He waved to a neighbour and petted his dog. He let his mind wander back over the past few months, feeling every bit as strange and out of bodied as he had when he first found the book. The mysterious author of those messages felt close to him now; somehow, strangely, as if he could sense him inside. Again he asked silently: why no clue? Why no clue about the thrombosis in the calf? It would have been so easy to add it later, to the post-death months, as a warning, why no clue? It could have been averted. She could be here, now. And then it came to him, so suddenly that it stopped him dead in his tracks. And he turned and hobbled with his stick back home as fast as he could.

He went upstairs without even bothering to remove his coat, only pausing in the study to collect his fountain pen. He picked up the pole with the brass hook and pulled down the wooden door in the ceiling. He unfolded the ladder and let the safety catch click into place. He climbed up as best he could – slower this time, but still able. He flicked the switch to illuminate the bulb and crawled over to the chimney breast. He knelt back and lifted the board, giddy with this plan, this plan that would protect all future Rogers from the horrible fate that had befallen him and the however many that had gone before. *He* would make the change. *He* would leave the clue. *He* would be the Roger that took care of all the Rogers and Rosemarys to come, into eternity. He rolled back the fibre glass insulation, not caring about his hands this time, and pulled at the board beneath. He didn't have the patience to fish about underneath it, and so he yanked at it instead, leaning back on his heels as he did so. The board was nailed in further back and so he had to pull hard. One good tug should do it, he thought. And that was the last thing he thought, as the whole board suddenly came up in his hands and he flew backwards, hitting his head with a sickening crack on a slanting wooden rafter.

Ten days later, James and Polly let themselves into the house. Despite the cold, the smell greeted them on the doorstep.

'Dad?' James called, wishing he had checked in on his father mid-week, as he clearly hadn't been washing himself or anything else for the past few days. The house was quiet. 'Stay here,' James told Polly and she nodded, quite happy to remain in the fresh air. James followed the stench up the stairs. He put his head round the bedroom door, and then the bathroom door and then the spare room-cum-study door, where the smell was most powerful. The ladder was an unwelcome but irresistible invitation and with his sleeve over his face, James climbed it.

The police said the cold had probably preserved Roger's body for a little while, but thought he had been dead at least a week. They said the cause of death was an acute trauma to the head and would have been almost immediate. They were baffled as to what he was doing in the loft, although it appeared that he had been looking for something under the floorboards next to the chimney breast, as he had ripped up the floor there. What he was looking for was a mystery, as the space under the boards was quite empty, but on closer inspection they had found a nest of mice which may have been making noises in the bedroom wall and annoying him. There were a lot of mice, the police had said, thousands of them, all exactly the same, blindly scrabbling around in the walls.

RICHARD HERRING

WOOLBOY

THE FOLLOWING IS a true story...

Tired of London, but still very much enjoying being alive (screw you, Doctor Samuel Johnson, you dead idiot) I had caught a train to Hertfordshire. I was going to walk in the woods, breathe fresh air, listen to birdsong and be alone with my thoughts.

It's strange the way that we assume that the countryside holds none of the dangers of the city and that being alone makes you more secure than being surrounded by millions of people. In Hertfordshire, just like in space, no one can hear you scream.

I fancied that I was returning to nature, somehow communing with the past, recapturing the simple and idyllic life of the noble ancient Britons. In truth, I suspect our ancestors didn't have much time for a nature ramble, being concerned mainly with fighting off invaders, disease and wild animals. They would probably have given their right arms to be able to escape nature completely. If you gave them the choice between living in a wood and my grotty flat in Shepherd's Bush I don't think they'd have to think twice about it. But I didn't let these facts shatter my illusions of the mythical notions of our Celtic past, even if I was just allowing myself to become a member of what was essentially a medieval version of UKIP.

I allowed myself the fantasy, because I deserved the break from reality. I had been working much too hard. Days and weeks and months of my life had disappeared without me noticing them, like pages of a day-by-day calendar being ripped off by an invisible hand in a shonkily filmed 1950s movie about time travel. Now unencumbered by deadlines and bulging inboxes I could stop and smell the roses, or in this case the musty combination of dead leaves and animal shit of the forest.

My senses sharp and vivid, I had the time to observe and enjoy the world around me: the way my shoe sunk into the damp earth, insects scurrying around the surprisingly life-like corpse of a fallen crow, the grotesque, yet alluring sight of a tree felled by lightning, its blackened, splintered trunk hopefully reaching upwards, as if it was unaware that its branches and leaves were gone. Something scampered through the leaves behind me and shot into a hole in the ground, as if fleeing from some unseen predator, its fear hanging palpably in the air.

For months I had barely noticed the sky above my head, but now my eyes had become an electron microscope and could zoom in on a single petal or a dew drop on a leaf; my hearing had taken on superhero proportions and I could pick out the helium buzz of an individual midge. I felt relaxed for the first time in months, yet primed for any attack by a sabre-toothed tiger or mammoth that might be lurking in this ancient part of Albion. My imagination has not been checked for historical accuracy.

The ground in front of me dipped and I stumbled, but stopped myself falling. Even though there was no one to see me, I carried out the whole self-conscious, dignity-restoring pantomime of pretending that the incident had never occurred, then looked down imagining some outside force had been responsible for the whole thing. Then I progressed gingerly down the slope.

The house was so well hidden amongst the trees that I didn't see it until I was only a few feet away. I wasn't expecting to see a habitation so deep into the woods and perhaps my eyes had been focused on tiny details so weren't ready to take in a large two-storey farmhouse. And the moment I had unscrambled the situation in my brain I was sent into a paroxysm of shock that saw me slipping backwards and falling on to my arse. A shadowy figure was seemingly staring out at me from the front window, its arms raised above its head.

I performed an ungracious bum shuffle as half my brain told me to flee and the other half was instructing me to get to my feet and consequently there was frenetic movement, but I stayed more or less where I was.

But fear turned to laughter as I glanced back at the window and properly saw what had spooked me. I lay down, relieved and shook my head. It wasn't a person. It was a doll. Not just an ordinary doll, a hand-knitted, life-size representation of a boy of about ten years old. His skin was bright pink, his hair made from brown flaxen strands and he had a massive comedic, yet demonic, smile stitched from ear to ear. He had both arms raised above his head as if he was banging on the window.

My laughter caught in my throat a bit. It wasn't a furious madman, but this was still a strange thing to behold. It was hard to process why this woolly monstrosity had been made at all, yet alone placed in this position.

The doll was wearing a real boy's clothes – they hadn't been knitted, but maybe bought from a shop or stolen from a dead child. Or a living child. I don't know why my mind went straight to that morbid possibility. They might have been stolen from a sleeping child . . . Actually that's rather more sinister. It conjures up the image of some stranger creeping into a child's bedroom at night, spiriting their clothes away and the confused infant waking in the morning, unable to get dressed, wondering where his pants are.

I was clearly spooked, but considering Woolboy more carefully did not assuage my fears. What the fuck was going on here?

The windows of the house were barred. Was that to keep burglars out or the lanate child within? Were the owners of this house afraid that some international soft toy thief might want to break into their abode to spirit away this wonky abomination? Or were the bars there for our protection? Without them would this junior Guy Fawkes smash through the window with his mitten hands and run amok, strangling the populace with his loose threads?

My imagination was running wild, but unless Woolboy comes alive when everyone is asleep (and for the moment I wasn't discounting that as a possibility) then someone had deliberately knitted him and then placed him in their own window, seemingly pleading to escape, which was actually slightly more unsettling than lifeless material self-animating.

I decided to get out of this weird place as quickly as I could, jumped to my feet and scurried through the leaves and twigs. At the back of the house was a narrow muddy track with tyre marks cut into it, that I presumed led to the main road. The house had an unpaved and empty driveway with a sign next to it saying 'Don't even *think* of parking here!'

I thought that was unnecessarily aggressive. We were in the middle of nowhere. I don't think anyone would think of parking there. Unless there was a sign expressly forbidding them from parking there, in which case they would have to think about parking there. It's a sign you have to disobey the minute you've read it. You can't read it and not on some level think about parking there. Whoever put that up must know that. They know you have broken their rule if you are aware of its existence. Presumably if you nonchalantly drove in without seeing the sign it wouldn't be a problem. 'Did you think about parking there?'

'No, I just drove in without thinking.'

'Right, well that's OK then . . . are you thinking about parking there now?'

'Well I am *now*.'

This whole place gave up the unsmellable stink of craziness. Instinct told me to get away from there as soon as possible. I didn't really even think about where I was going. Perhaps common sense should have sent me back the way I came, or at least along the muddy road that led to civilization. But I blundered forwards deeper into the wood.

And I was now thinking of something that hadn't crossed my mind for three decades. I had felt this fear before in almost identical circumstances. When I was fourteen I'd been on a school trip to Devon and been walking in the woods with a few of my classmates. We'd come across an isolated farmhouse hidden in the trees, with a similar air of sorrow and loneliness. There were dolls in the window of that house too. Is that a thing? If you decide you're going to live alone in the middle of a forest is there something that clicks inside you and says, 'Right, well, better sort some dolls out for the windows, then.' These ones weren't knitted, but bought from a shop, yet still in their boxes, still in their cellophane. These three dolls stared out from the three upstairs windows. Because if you've bought some dolls to decorate your house you don't think, 'I'll put those looking into my bedroom so I can enjoy them,' you think, 'I'll place those staring out into the woods like they're evil sentinels ready to launch themselves at any overly curious teenagers.' There was a Christmas tree in the lounge even though it was June. And that house had a weird warning sign too. On the door it said, 'Beware of the very viscous Alsatian'.

We were over-confident and clever-clever swots, so we laughed heartily at this mistake. But one of us suggested, 'Maybe there's really a very watery dog in there.'

'Yes, if you break in it will come running at you, jump up and explode into a pool of Alsatian gloop – how will I get this out of my clothes?'

'You don't even have to break in. A viscous dog can sense you're outside and then slide out under the front door like a canine Terminator.'

'He might even be a friendly dog. It's just a warning not to pet him. Please don't stroke our viscous dog, you'll disturb the surface tension.'

We had walked away laughing, but I had been chilled by this house and later wrote a bad teenage poem trying to guess who lived in this place, which I described tellingly as 'lonely as a mind'.

Back in the present day and the house and Woolboy were five minutes behind me and I was already starting to find the situation and my own petrified reaction slightly amusing. Clearly some eccentric granny had knitted the child and then maybe placed it in that position as a joke, or as a greeting to their own grandchild (though what kind of grandmother would live in such an inaccessible location?). But even though wool is not the best medium for creating human expression I couldn't shake the feeling that the face had been forlorn and pitiful. Pleading maybe. For a second I thought I should return to the house and free this imprisoned cuddly toy. I was being ridiculous of course and I ploughed blindly onwards.

Then I stopped. In front of me on the path was a big black dog. I don't know the breed, but the kind that you sometimes see scary men dragging along on a piece of string. It was much wider than it was tall, and had huge haunches, like it spent three hours a day in the doggy gym. It was standing there, looking at me, panting and displaying its teeth, which looked vicious, though the drool emanating from its jowls did give them the appearance of viscosity as well.

The dog had a collar on, so I expected to see its owner rounding the corner at any moment and calling it to heel. But no one appeared. The dog looked at me as if daring me to move. I stayed still and looked back, ready to flee if it tried to run-waddle at me.

After what felt like minutes a tall, thin middle-aged man in a flat cap slunk out of the shadows. He didn't acknowledge me, no friendly greeting, not even a nod. He just walked by me, a little too close, with the dog following.

Just as he got behind me the man stopped stock-still

and started fishing in his pocket for something. Now I was properly terrified. Was this the man who owned the house? Had he knitted the boy? Was he looking at me and thinking, 'He's thinking about parking in my parking space. I warned him not to. Why is he doing that? He has to die.'

In this moment I was convinced he was a serial killer. Perhaps his gimmick was to knit his victims in their last seconds. The ten-year-old boy had made it to the window but no further, the bars blocking his escape. Maybe the whole house was a woolly mausoleum, with yarn-based effigies of the terrified dead in every corner. I wondered if the mummified remains of the unfortunate dead lay inside these handmade sarcophagi. Was this man, faceless due to the shadows cast by the peak of his cap, reaching for his needles and a ball of wool? Was his dog about to jump on me and envelop me in a watery sphere that I could not escape from, which would roll me back to the house where my remains would rest, encased in sheep fur, until the authorities finally stumbled across this museum of death and knitting?

I'd have given anything to be back in Shepherd's Bush at this moment. We've got knife crime, we've got feral children swearing at you for going about your business, we've got tramps openly shitting on the pavement in broad daylight. But there are not Woolboys battering on windows and there are plenty of people around to hear you if you scream.

For whatever reason the man in the woods let me live that day. I think he might just have sized me up, realised he hadn't brought quite enough wool to craft my somewhat stocky frame.

I broke into a jog and then a run and emerged from

the woods and headed straight for the train station and my home. If you go down to the woods today, you might not be so lucky.

TIM KEY

HALLOWEEN

RICHARD DECIDED TO give his missus a fright on Halloween night.

He chopped his head off and hid it in the freezer.[1]

But by the time she opened the freezer he was so weak he could barely say 'Boo!'

And there was that much blood on the ready meals her main emotion was one of fury.

---

1 I'm thinking here about a freezer like the one we used to have in our garage or like the one the thugs put a man into in the film *Shallow Grave*. A chest freezer, I think is its technical name. The one in our garage had things like frozen casseroles and pizzas in it. Sometimes I'd put on shoes if I had to go to the garage and get something from the freezer and other times I'd go in just my socks. You had to walk sideways to get past the car.

RUFUS HOUND

FIXED

NOTHING.

Nothing at all.

Then, very suddenly, not nothing.

Waking up has prerequisites – chief amongst them that, initially, something is asleep. This wasn't that. Nothing had been asleep, and yet, here, now, something was awake. It was confusing. From absence to presence, from zero to one, from death to life – how? Why? Where? *Whatwhatwhatwhat*? *Who*?

Mere moments ago there was nothing capable of asking a question – of even understanding the concept of questions and yet, now, too many of them; complete incomprehension, bombarded by a screaming desperation for answers, for any speck of information that would make some – *any* – part of this make sense. Like waking up whilst drowning, but with death as its genesis, rather than its feared conclusion.

A sound.

Senses jangle, dulled, but suddenly focused on this single, perceivable thing. And again. A sound. Like a ball of waxed paper collapsing in on itself, a pause, then its sonic antonym, that crushed thing expanding – or rather struggling to expand; the air needed to fill it, dawdling; not rushing. To nullify the vacuum with a long, slow wheeze. These are not reassuring sounds. Whatever answers they lead to are the kind that make the question wish it hadn't been asked ('What do you mean 'She just disappeared'?', 'You were screwing him *the entire time*?', 'Are you sure it's cancer?'). And again.

And again.

Something is breathing. Something is struggling to breathe. You.

Were it not for everything else, maybe the oddness of that realisation would stab home harder; that, for a moment, you existed outside of matter – a ghost, a temporary angel – but no longer. Now, you return to being, the formerly abandoned machinery within, pressed once more to function. Redundant nerve endings now re-employed, each dendrite ferociously awakening, furious, meting out barbs of white hot pain, a biological 'fuck you' to the impossibility of your current situation. As the circuitry of your central nervous system shrieks into operation, your brain floods with frantic feedback. Pain. Such incredible pain, blood replaced by broken glass. You'd cry out but the best you can manage is a short, wheezing moan as legs and arms spasm, joining the torture chorus with fresh verses of their own.

Hands, thumbs, fingers all log in, the electricity jolting through them, heralding their connection to this . . . body? Person? Yes. Yes! That's right! You are – were – human. These are human things, aren't they? Hands, legs . . . people have those! The fragile thought is almost drowned by the merciless anguish, but you cling to it. You are a person. You are a person who is on fire? It feels like it, but no. No flame. No smoke. The burning's internal, inextinguishable, a thing to be endured.

You endure it, terrified. Not just of the pain, but that the pain might cast out what little knowledge has been won. How long will it last? How long has it been going? Questions pop like sparks from an open fire, but fizzle out just as quickly. You have no space for them. With nothing to do but wait – alone, blind, ravaged – you wait.

Minutepainhourpaindaypainmonthpainyearpain. You wait.

Throbbingsearingtearingstabbingboilingbursting. You wait.

And then, at some point, it fades. Whatever terrible thing visited you, it's leaving, new details strewn in its wake. You're a person. You're . . . lying down? In the dark? No . . . inside . . . something? Devoid of context or intellect, each thought exists alone. Stringing these together, weaving sense from these thin strands of knowing, is beyond you. Though increasingly less so. You take a deep breath, immediately regretting the effort, as you fill with thick, foetid air; your newly operational lungs ill-prepared for the onslaught. Deep, wrenching coughs crack through aching muscles, punch through heart, lungs, ribs. More coughing, more pain, stars seen.

You try again. Where are you? New, old fingers feel plush, cushioned softness. Stretching is impossible, in any direction. A soft cell, not much bigger than yourself. That's where you are, now wh–

Lightning. Pure white, blindingly so, striking from within, your brain full of it, spiking with sincere violence. No thoughts, nothing other than a billion bright burning banshees, an unholy choir of light and pain, an opera of a million migraines. You thrash. It continues. You continue. It doesn't care.

At some point it ends, and in ending, the first of its gifts is revealed.

You can cry.

How could this happen to you? You're dead. You died. You remember.

You *remember*.

Your full autobiography, pages disordered, the story fragmented, chapter titles, paragraphs, photographs, glimpses of the path that lead to this, this . . . coffin. The cuttings begin to order themselves and the cerebral slideshow begins.

Drizzle. Cold. Bare brick walls and kin already sick of them. A fug of trudging drudgery waiting for you to come of age; that its slog of grim, respectless toil may claim you too. Automaton sickness masquerading as life. This is all there is for you. Their sadness, your future.

The only softness, her. What part duty, what part love? Irrelevant. Love. Respite in her bosom, safety in her arms. Did she know? As you were pulled from her into the world, did she realise she had birthed a titan? That her job was to conceal you while you grew strong enough. To stand guard over your potential, to protect you from the big boys. To hide you. So important to hide.

Manhood, and ditched humility. That which doesn't kill us and all that, yeah? A lion should roar. Everything's changing, but that's good. Change. Be different. Rock and Roll! Pretty girls! Fucking Teddy Boys. There's a power to that music. It stirs things up, lets the lightest and brightest float to the top, and you are *so* light; so beneficial, emptiness.

Oh, your beautiful rise! From the shit on their shoes to the jewel in their crown. Master of his own path, usurper of fate. Who could resist a man so much bigger than destiny? No one. Come Kings! Come Queens! Come the great and the good! Usher forth the lowly, that they too might gaze upon this knight's divinity! *Come keepers of secrets!*

Such delicious secrets. The secrets of an untouchable man. Of tears snaking down plump, young cheeks. You don't bother putting a hand over their mouths. They could scream, but the sheer disbelief of anyone hearing it would render any sound mute. If they ran, who would they run to? Who would dare entertain such vile lies, so clearly borne of jealousy, or a broken home, or mental illness? You had fashioned your disguise perfectly. A man of such permanent, beneficent sacrifice, a common man of royal approval – a man of music! Not for one second could anyone consider that such a man might be busily raping an inhuman opus through the small, the vulnerable and the dead; a thought so sickening that the world would rather blindly refute it than engage with its possibility. A monster pointing at the ceiling, before slithering back under the bed. So important to hide.

Whilst you escaped their accusations you never quite escaped your humanity. Though not for the lack of trying. There was always 'that' moment. That dreaded few seconds of self-awareness as the semen finished pumping its way into the defiled thing. That rush of orgasm, ruined by a concurrent wave of guilt and horror. Every victory rendered hollow by that tiny voice inside, screaming at you to stop. Not that you ever would. If there was one thing you had mastered, it was the ability to ignore tiny voices screaming 'Stop!'. You had trusted that it would only be a matter of time before that internal protest was permanently quashed, imploding under the weight of its own futility. Exorcising that sliver of spoiling shame would allow you to enjoy each conquest, untarnished.

It was the thing you wanted most, but – alas – the one thing you never managed. In truth, the wretchedness increased each time, and the more years and victims that amassed behind you, the harder it was to wade free from the tarry pools of mortification. If you let your mind wander, sometimes your gut would clench and your breathing would fail as the guilt blindsided you. To be so utterly appalled by yourself, yet so proud of having shrugged off whatever version of 'normal' it is that damns cowards to small, servile lives. Running was the only balm. So you ran. And ran. And ran – your disguise so perfect that no one ever asked just what it was you were running *from*.

And now, the realisation. There's nowhere to run. Not in here. No distractions of any kind. Now there's just you and the tiny voices, hundreds of them. Sobbing. Screaming. Begging. Tortured sounds of stolen innocence. Howls of despair. You try screaming yourself, but there's more of them and they're louder. There's no sound you can make that will drown out this anguished chorale; nowhere to look that you might distract yourself from the clammy faces, the furrowed brows and wet eyes, glinting repositories of violation and betrayal. All yours.

All yours.

You scream. You shout. You cry. You thrash. For as long as this continues, what else could you possibly do?

The man in the raincoat looked out of the window as the old lady gathered her things. 'Did it work?' he asked.

'We'll never know for certain. Short of digging him up,' she chuckled. 'And that would rather ruin the effect, wouldn't it? But from what I can tell, yes.'

'So, he's alive? Right now?'

'Not *alive*, per se. Just not dead. If he was alive, he might die again. And we can't have that, can we? Not ever.'

DANIELLE WHEELER

IN LOVING MEMORY OF NERYS BAG

NERYS BAG AWOKE in total darkness. Her head was pounding. Each heartbeat making her wince as her thick, sticky blood coursed its way to her fragile brain. She felt clammy, her back as wet as her mouth was dry. Reaching beneath the ratty blanket that covered her, Nerys realised she was still fully clothed. Relief washed over her. 'I'm going to be really late for work,' she thought, as she vomited over her alarm clock.

As it turned out, Nerys was only fifteen minutes late for work that morning, having decided against a shower and grabbing a can of Relentless and three bags of Monster Munch from the newsagents for breakfast. Nerys knew someday soon she'd need to take a long hard look at her life. But she wasn't going to do it today as she felt like shit and it was her occasional friend's hen weekend soon and she planned to get absolutely wankered then. But after the wedding maybe she'd start saving again for a deposit on a nicer flat, rather than stay in her crappy bedsit with its tiny window and mouse problem. Nerys could only ever afford places with mice. She was certain that's why she needed to sleep with her pants on. 'What if a mouse got in there and laid . . . baby mice? Mice don't lay eggs do they . . . ?'

Once at work, Nerys started her usual morning routine of deleting emails without even reading them before being jolted from her banal and frankly idiotic train of thought about mice eggs: the date at the bottom of the screen. Today? How had it not registered? She'd not really thought about it for years, dismissed it as a stupid childish prank. But today's date, those were the numbers that as a teenager had terrified her. 'It hadn't even crossed my mind . . .'

'Talking to yourself again?' Candy was the only other person in the office. Everyone else was more important so they were always in meetings . . . probably. Nerys assumed they were in meetings. She didn't really know to be honest. There might have been a memo once but she more than likely didn't read it.

'Fuck off,' replied Nerys.

When Candy first started working at the homeless charity Nerys couldn't even speak to her, she was so in awe of the leggy blonde's beauty. But after three months she realised Candy was a complete prick and from then on, conversation flowed a lot easier. Nerys made herself a cup of tea and sat back at her desk. Staring at the date on the wall clock this time, an uneasy feeling crept up inside her. Starting in her stomach, passing through her chest and resting in her throat, like heavy concrete moths dancing in her digestive system. You see, when Nerys was fourteen years old she was told today would be the day she died.

Twelve years ago, Nerys Bag had been – what the kids at her comprehensive school called – 'a weirdo'. She wasn't really that weird, she just liked indie music, watched a lot of horror films and wore black jeans instead of the regulation blue. But in a school where everyone else listened to R&B, still watched telly and smoked pot, she supposed she was technically weird. 'Technically'.

One evening Nerys and her small band of fellow 'weirdos' thought it would be a lot of fun to sneak their way into a screening of *The Exorcist* and scare themselves until liquid came out (tears/nosebleeds/wee – anything goes). Marian swore it was the most frightening thing she'd ever seen. Even more frightening than that time her uncle had a seizure in Morrisons. She couldn't touch scones after that. The problem was, *The Exorcist* is not at all scary when viewed in a cinema surrounded by a hundred cynical teenagers who all think it's hilarious to see a child rubbing her bits with a crucifix before being sick on her own mother. Disappointed, they went back to Nerys's house looking for a cheap thrill. And they got it via the Ouija board they found in the cupboard under the stairs.

Marian, Katy, Nerys and their other friend Mo laid the board out on the kitchen table – Nerys's father had already gone to bed, knowing the little gang would be up all night chatting about hair and soap operas and quilts. No, he didn't really 'get' women. None of the girls knew what they were doing so they'd just lit some candles, held hands and called upon the spirits to communicate with them – just like they'd seen on telly – and waited.

Nothing.

Happened.

Marian was terrified; the other three, more amused at her fear than anything else. 'What was that noise?' she whispered.

'The wind? From my dad's bum?' Nerys and the others were in hysterics.

'Take it seriously!' cried Marian. 'They get angry if you laugh at them.' The three other girls suppressed their giggles enough to each place a finger on the upturned egg cup they used as the counter.

'I'll go first,' said Katy. 'Is there anyone there? And if so, please do tell us your name. Thank you. From Katy.'

'You're not dictating a telegram,' whispered Mo.

'What's a telegram?'

'Shush!' Marian interrupted the pair. 'Look.'

Sure enough, the egg cup started moving around the letters. 'H.U.G.H.'

'Hugh! His name is Hugh!'

'It's still going,' Mo said, looking at Katy and Nerys.

'J.N.U.S.' Marian's voice was trembling. 'We've made contact with Hugh J Nus . . . huge anus. Oh, very funny. I'm going home.'

Nerys stood up. 'Please don't. Look, let's do it properly this time.'

'Well . . . OK.' Nerys remembered they'd asked a few innocent questions, the egg cup whizzing round the board. None of them admitted to pushing it – she certainly wasn't – but she hadn't really believed they'd been in the presence of anything supernatural. Until Marian got brave that is.

'I've got a question. When will Nerys Bag die?'

'That's horrible,' cried out Mo.

'Are you scared, Nerys?' Marian asked. 'Shall we ask something else?'

'Ask what you like. It's all bollocks anyway.' Nerys took her hand away from the counter. Followed by Mo and Katy, until just Marian had a finger gently touching the ceramic pot.

Nothing happened nothing happened nothing happened.

The egg cup started to move towards the numbers at the far side of the board.

'This isn't funny, Marian,' said Katy.

'I'm not pushing it. I promise!' A look of genuine terror crossed Marian's face.

'Stop it!' cried Nerys. 'I'm sorry we laughed at you.'

'It isn't me!' Marian tried to move her finger away from the cup but something was stopping her. 'I can't move my hand!'

'Stop!' yelled Mo, leaping to her feet.

'I can't,' Marian was sobbing now as the counter got faster. Nerys didn't want to know, she tried to look away but her eyes remained glued to the egg cup making its way around the kitchen table, repeating the date over and over and over until . . . everything stopped. Marian pulled her hand away and ran upstairs to the bathroom. Nerys was in a state of shock. The three sat in silence for what felt like an hour. (Seven minutes.)

Finally, Katy spoke.

'She was playing a trick on us? Wasn't she?'

'Yeah,' said Mo. 'A trick.'

Nerys looked at her two best friends. Neither of them sounded convinced. But she could tell they wanted her to reassure them. She was the smart one. She was doing double science in her GCSEs.

'Yeah. A trick.'

They never spoke of that night again. Not for spooky reasons – a week later they found out Katy had been shagging Mo's boyfriend behind her back. Mo was devastated in only a way a fourteen-year-old virgin can be, and the close-knit little group of friends never really hung out again.

So now here Nerys was. On the day that had been chanted by an egg cup twelve years ago. Nerys didn't even believe in ghosts anyway, stupid idiot ghosts.

'What's up, babes?' Candy sounded genuinely concerned. Which was a first for her.

'Nothing. I'm hungover.' Nerys immediately regretted saying she was hungover. Why didn't she say food poisoning and take the afternoon off?

'No, babes. You look really, really, really shit. Not hungover,' Candy grabbed Nerys's face and stared at her, examining every inch of skin.

'You look like you're dying.'

Nerys rushed to the bathroom and looked in the mirror over the sink. It was a unisex bathroom so the mirror was hung just a tiny bit too high for her five foot stature. But she saw enough of her eyes to know she looked exactly the same as she always did. Not great, admittedly, but five-a-day is expensive and she had booze to buy. Nerys stormed to the kitchen where Candy was making a low-calorie Cup-a-Soup.

'Bitch!'

'It was a joke!'

But Nerys wasn't in the mood. She hesitated, thinking of the correct punishment, before punching Candy's mug out of her hand.

'That's my best mug! It's from the Isle of Wight! Look: Cowes you can't milk, Needles you can't thread . . .'

Nerys returned to her desk. She slumped down. Confused.

'Candy. Do you believe in ghosts?'

'What? First you punch my best mug ever out of my hands and now you're asking me about ghosts? What's wrong with you?'

'I'm sorry about the mug.'

Candy finally realised something was troubling Nerys. She softened, perching her amazing arse next to Nerys's stapler.

'I've never told anyone this. Ever. But yes. I did see something. Once.'

'You're crapping me up,' Nerys often made up her own lingo. It was one of her quirks.

'No. I really did. I was about five years old. It was winter, the ground was white. It was so cold it took your breath away. I'd been sent to bed early for being a 'pathetic dick'. I heard a noise outside. A terrifying whisper. I was scared but I needed to know what it was . . .'

Nerys was barely breathing. Candy continued.

'I looked out of my bedroom window and saw him. Sat there silently in the snow. He looked up at me with his big coal-like eyes and long carroty nose. It was amazing.'

Nerys vowed that if she didn't die today she'd definitely kill Candy once this month's audit had been done.

Later that afternoon, Nerys started to feel much calmer about the whole thing. She'd downloaded an 'antianxiety' app and had turned the radio from some local bullshit station that played Pharrell too often, to Classic FM. She liked listening to Classic FM. There would always be some point in the afternoon where you could pretend you were in *Superman* or *Jurassic Park* or *Jaws*. So peaceful and relaxing. Nerys always thought she'd be in a movie someday. A real one. Not like the one she had to get taken off of YouTube of her wearing 'tops no bottoms', pretending to ride a static washing line. Proper movies starring people with verified Twitter accounts. In her heart she thought she could still be an actor. She just needed to join a local group, maybe make a short film. Send it out to some agents. She just wanted to shift those last few pounds off her thighs before she'd feel really comfortable in front of the camera. Yes, that was her plan. She needed to lose a bit of weight, join an AmDram group, meet some young film-makers and then she'd probably be in *Hollyoaks* within twelve months. And in Hollywood in two years. But maybe she wanted to go back to university? She'd dropped out after getting gout at the end of her first year. She always wanted to be an astronaut. And in some ways she thought she probably still could be. She'd just get her degree, learn French and German, apply for a job at the European Space Agency (she had worked at the Leicester Space Centre for six months while her Nan was dying so her CV was already quite impressive), so within five years she could start her astronaut training. Although maybe she should learn French and German first? Do an evening class? Yes, she'd do that. In September. No point starting in the middle of the academic year.

Nerys was ripped from her thoughts by . . . she didn't know what. She looked around the office, not even

Candy was here. She'd gone home early because her cat was sick. Though come to think of it, who had texted Candy about the cat? Not the cat itself. Dirty lies!

Nerys was once again interrupted by something . . . but it wasn't a noise. She felt as if her soul was being invaded by an army of jackbooted soldiers made of Play-Doh. As if something was slicing into her and climbing inside. However, it wasn't painful. It was sort of wonderful but horrific at the same time. Like having acupuncture. As soon as the sensation started, it was over. And then it came, wave after wave, a convulsion of indescribable terror and joy. When it finally stopped she felt as if she'd just vomited herself to an orgasm. Her heart was racing, she was freezing cold. This was doing nothing for her hangover. She looked up the symptoms on the internet but could find nothing for 'Play-Doh men dancing in your soul'. The cold sweats however suggested she might not have eaten enough lunch. Nerys stood up to make her way to the communal fridge and promptly blacked out.

When Nerys awoke, the office was pitch black except for the tiny flicker of her screen saver and the faint dots from a variety of electrical items put on standby rather than powered down. (So bad for the environment.) She'd been on the floor for three hours. Even Nerys, with her relaxed attitude to personal safety, knew this wasn't good. But she was feeling OK and she'd not got round to registering with a GP, although she'd lived in the area for six years.

'If it happens again I'll definitely go to hospital or something,' she thought to herself.

Now, most people after such a weird and frightening experience would have called someone. A parent, a sibling, a lover, a best friend. Nerys had none of these. Not anymore. She was pretty proud of being able to take care of herself, although it was a situation circumstance had thrust upon her rather than one she chose. She wouldn't allow herself to think about it. It's the only way to stay strong. Just go home, watch five episodes of *RuPaul's Drag Race*, and call it a night.

As soon as Nerys stepped outside the office door, as soon as she'd set the alarm and triple locked the heavy front door, she felt as if she was being watched. It was so intense she couldn't quite believe no one was with her. She could almost, *almost* see someone. A shadow in her periphery but not even a shadow. A shadow of a shadow of something that wasn't there. She took a deep breath and started the fifteen-minute walk home. Was it her imagination or was it darker this evening? Maybe some of the streetlights were off? The night felt as if it had been dipped in treacle. Every step took enormous effort, but as soon as she thought about the motion, the movement of joint and muscle, the sticky feeling dissipated. The eyes on her though, they remained.

She quickened her pace, she slowed down, she walked past three different fried chicken shops. Nerys even popped into the local cinema to see what was coming out at the weekend. And yet the only constant was the feeling she was being watched. And not from afar. Not some pervert with night vision goggles peering at her from behind a bush as he tugged his winkle to climax. No. Eyes attached to a face that was breathing hot air on to her neck. Nerys turned excruciatingly slowly, as if whatever was behind her might disappear with any sudden movement. As she moved she caught her reflection in a darkened shop window. She looked terrified. And yet there was nothing there.

The sense of relief that crashed over Nerys as she raced up the stairs to her cramped bedsit and slammed the door shut was palpable. Unfortunately it lasted merely seconds before the eyes without a face bore into her once more. The feeling of dread and horror, of being watched, that something was waiting, became too much for her. She went to her bathroom and opened the mirrored cupboard over the sink. Staring at the few bottles in there, she didn't even know what she was looking for. Was she going to overdose? No, of course not. So what was she planning? Nerys started to close the door but stopped herself. What if the thing that has followed her, that was looking at her, was in the mirror? She'd be face to face with whatever it was that was making her heart feel like it was about to burst from her chest. She shut her eyes and slammed the cupboard door with such force that the mirror smashed into the sink. Holding up one of the larger shards, she stared directly at herself, before turning the angle to see what was behind her. Nothing. There was nothing there.

Nerys shook as she sat on her sofa clutching the shattered mirror in her hand. The oppressive impression of being under surveillance was too much.

'Leave me alone.'

She waved the glass at nothing in particular, the feeling growing more intense with each swipe. It was as if whatever had been looking at her was now in her personal space. Half in her, half out, nesting in the bed it had prepared in her body earlier at the office. What had earlier been a sensation was full blown crippling pain now. Had the Ouija board been right? Was today the day she died? But there was nothing there. Suddenly feeling brave, feeling absolutely certain she was going to find this . . . whatever, she stood up and started to search the room, overturning the table, tearing down the curtain, smashing the TV screen.

Nothing. No one. Not even a mouse.

She sat back down on her sofa and pulled a blanket around herself. If no one was here, who was looking at her?

The answer to that question was easily answered if she'd just opened her eyes a little wider. If she'd given in to the fear. That look of horror on the face of a corpse. That's how wide she needed to open her eyes to see the young man, wearing all black, sat next to her. He'd been with her all day. He felt sad she had ignored him, had dismissed his attempts to love her. He took her hand and held it tight. Nerys turned her head towards the tiny window of her tiny bedsit where she kept a framed photo of her parents. It was the last thing Nerys Bag ever saw.

PHILL JUPITUS

ANTHEMOESSA

'You muppet, Staples, that's never a fucking gram!' said Mike.

As he stood shoulder to shoulder in the cramped cubicle with the two other men, Steve Webb felt an old familiar warmth creeping up his neck and across his cheeks. This moment was one that he had imagined often since first starting in mergers and acquisitions and he was most put out that it wasn't anything like as exotic or rock and roll as he had seen in all the films. In *Scarface*, which Steve watched for the first time two weeks ago, Al Pacino stands wild eyed and wired in front of a pile of cocaine generous enough to kill an elephant. The small hillock of pure white powder put Steve in mind of *The Great British Bake Off*. At the time, he remembered thinking that he wouldn't have been surprised if Pacino had set down his machine gun before cracking three eggs into the pile while Sue Perkins arches her eyebrows saying, 'Three eggs! Well it looks like Tony Montana certainly means business with this Battenburg . . .'

'Don't be a cunt, Mike! At least he's gone and got some.' The voice of Jon Phelps managed to halt the reddening on Steve's now mercifully cooling cheeks. Since starting at work Steve had found Jon to be one of the few men who seemed to like him. Not that this was in any way a certainty, but what he did know was that Jon treated him less like a dick than everybody else.

Steve hadn't been shocked by what he had encountered when he started work. The world of high finance had barely been dented by the incredibly public financial scandals of the previous six years. The world had been brought to its knees by the insanely cavalier wheeler dealing of the financial sector. The government made all the right noises about regulation and putting controls in place to the press, but it became rapidly apparent that all they would ever really do is make noises. Every time you saw Cameron or Osborne on telly talking with their 'serious frowny' faces about controls within the financial services industry, the only thing that was missing at the end of each statement was the colossal wink to their old school mates who owned the fuckers.

Growing up in Essex and drinking in the bars around Fenchurch Street station whenever he came up to London for a jolly, he had seen swarms of these brash, sharp-suited men standing around and barking at each other for years. The noise they made as a group was always a little louder than you heard in any other pub, a little more *feral*. Whenever he heard their laughter it was violent, brash and utterly joyless. But curiously, he found himself wishing that he could laugh like that at somebody one day. To be stood in one of those groups of men and laughing at the misfortune of someone else. Not to be the one being laughed at would be a refreshing change of pace for Steve Webb.

His mates at sixth form had mostly gone on to university, but Steve always knew he wanted to work in the Square Mile. Nothing else would do. And so he began writing to hundreds of companies while he was still doing his A-levels. Any kind of job would do, he just needed to get through the door and then could take matters from there. He signed up with every employment agency along Bishopsgate, scoured the internet and pestered friends with parents in the business. And that was how, when he was eighteen, he started as a delivery clerk in the stationery department of J.D. Penrose.

His job was curiously anachronistic for such a mercilessly high-tech industry. He would deliver pens, pencils and Post-Its to all the departments of J.D.P. The stationery warehouse was located away from the main buildings, in the warren of lanes just east of Old Street. He would make four or five tours of the main buildings each day, come rain or shine. Sometimes there would be a 'special', which he would have to fill out immediately and run across.

Making deliveries for such a massive organisation gave him a unique overview of the whole structure. A full circuit of the two buildings would take him an hour and ten minutes depending on how many departments had ordered. He'd always begin in the bowels of the post room and then up to reception and security on ground and then up to where he really wanted to be: the floors.

For such a vast operation the department he worked in was quite modestly staffed. George Hughes was the stationery manager and had been with Penrose since he was Steve's age. He was a tiny wiry man with a slicked back mop of slate grey hair, rarely at his desk because he would be at the loading dock smoking. Pretty much all of his duties were conducted from the loading dock in order to facilitate his habit. George's number two was Terry Moss an imposing northerner who Steve thought might have been a miner at some point in the past. This was never really certain as Steve couldn't understand a word that Terry said. This was not ideal as it was Terry's job to show him where all the various departments were. As they pushed the trolley along the corridors Terry would gesture at certain doorways arching his eyebrows and frowning or chuckling like a large avuncular bear.

Over the coming months Steve got to know every single corridor and room of J.D. Penrose. He knew the names of everybody on staff and which departments they worked for. One thing that struck him about the geography of high finance was the way that the buildings got quieter the higher you went up them. The trading floors were like Bedlam. Mergers and acquisitions was no less manic but just a bit quieter and somehow more assured. This pattern of diminishing volume repeated itself right the way up to the chairman's floor, which was quiet as a graveyard. He was always polite and cheery and within three months had even gained a nickname, 'Staples', given to him by Jon Phelps on perhaps his fifth visit to mergers and acquisitions.

Steve's long-term game plan was gradually coming together. He was on a nodding basis with the heads of every department. He had felt confident enough on several occasions to actually have football discussions with some of them. Harsh, testosterone-fuelled banter was the order of the day. The energy was intense and everybody seemed grimly aware that you not only had to be good at your job, but you also had to be able to hold your own in the pub afterwards. You worked hard, talked fast, but played harder. And if you couldn't hack it, then you would perish almost immediately. Steve's easy manner and the non-threatening nature of his position meant that any room he walked into immediately co-opted him as an arbitrator in some or other petty dispute.

'Oy, Staples, is this tie blue or green?'

'Oy, Staples, would you rather shag Cheryl Cole now, or when she was first in Girls Aloud?'

'Oy, Staples, how many Jägerbombs do you think Jackson could do before he'd pass out?'

After six months of careful consideration he had made up his mind. He was going to go to HR and apply to take an internal entry-level appointment board for a position in mergers and acquisitions. The internal promotion of staff had been a key aspect of life at J.D. Penrose. It was said that old man Penrose himself had been in the post room for two years before becoming a ledger clerk and then climbing the ladder to make J.D. Penrose one of the world's most prosperous financial operations. The part of the legend, which had been glossed over, was the fact that his dad, *old*-old man Penrose owned the bank anyway and had made his errant son work in the post room for two years after he got a secretary pregnant while he was still at Oxford.

Steve had been patiently gathering information over the previous months in preparation for this moment. And as he walked into his boardroom and sat at the table his heart leaped with joy to see that the two people opposite were Jean from HR and Jon Phelps. He had to fight to keep a straight face as Jon actually winked at him when Jean asked the question: 'So, Stephen. Why do you want to work in mergers and acquisitions?'

After a fairly low-level grilling which lasted a shade under twenty minutes, Jean offered a hand over the table and smiled, 'Welcome to mergers and acquisitions, Mister Webb.' Steve smiled and turned to Jon who handed him a manila folder.

'Well, Steve, everything you need to know is in this folder. We have already notified your department that you'll be starting with us in two weeks, and we look forward to having you on the team.' As Steve took the folder, Jon shook his hand, the grip just a little firmer than he had expected. He walked out of the room and headed for the lifts, pressing the button to call it. As the lift took him down he opened the folder Jon had given him. The front page contained the words:

J.D. PENROSE
MERGERS AND ACQUISITIONS

Underneath this was a small three-inch square Post-It note on which was written the words:

Don't fuck it up.

While not as savage as the trading floors below, mergers and acquisitions still hummed with a controlled urgency. Jon put Steve at a desk with Mike Taylor in order to be shown the ropes. This was a slight disappointment as Taylor was one of the older members of staff. At thirty-four he was fucking ancient for this game. He had moved up to M&A three years previously, after the reorganisation of the Hong Kong desk. He was full of all sorts of far-fetched stories about nights out he'd been on in the Far East, tales of expensive prostitutes and mounds of cocaine and exotic foods and incredible hotels. ''Fing is, Staples,' he slurred – Steve bridled a little at this. While everybody else now called him by his name, Taylor had persisted in addressing him by his old stationery department nickname. While this was basic-level gamesmanship it didn't make it any less annoying – "fing is, Staples, that when you get a bird in Hong Kong you fuckin' make sure that it is a bird. 'Cos I'm not fuckin' joking, the geezers out there who dress as birds look fuckin' well tasty. And if you've 'ad a few, well . . .' He let the sentence hang.

'Well what?' asked Steve.

'Mistakes may occur . . .' said Taylor, with an arch of the eyebrow.

It was at that moment Steve decided that he would see to it personally within the year that he would have this man's job. This relic. This dinosaur. Thirty-four fucking years old. It made Steve almost feel physically sick to imagine this waste of air rampaging around the Orient throwing cash at anybody who'd suck his cock. And that arch of the eyebrow said that he'd let a bloke do it. Steve nodded assent at this golden nugget of wisdom and turned back to his terminal while thinking, 'I will fucking end you, you piece of shit.'

But despite his slowly unfolding career plan Steve still had to play his cards right. Schmoozing colleagues at the weekend was all part of the game. You had to hold your own on a Friday night with the lads. Surprise them with generosity when it's your round – 'Jack Daniel's chasers, Webby, you fucking diamond!' But the dark currency of the Friday night bender was coke. The real wheeling and dealing of the social whirl of the Square Mile was conducted in the gents all clustered around a cistern top and a rolled-up twenty. There was a bloke on the Tokyo desk who always used a rolled-up 100 military yen note which was basically an antique from the Second World War. As he came up pinching his nostrils and squeezing his eyes closed he would usually make some quip like, 'And THAT is how we did it at Pearl Harbor!' before barging his way back to the bar.

Steve was aware that he had been dependent on others for his cocaine. He was unfamiliar with the etiquette. Can you just ask someone where they got it? Do you offer to buy it? Do you offer them a fiver if you have a line? It was not a world he was familiar with. After a few clumsily indiscreet enquiries he eventually discovered that there was a girl in the post room who was the conduit for nearly eighty per cent of the drugs coming in to the building. He had to be introduced to her by Mike Taylor, which was another reminder to destroy Taylor's life as swiftly as possible. He hated being beholden to him.

'Katie, this is the geezer I told you about, this is Staples, I shall leave you two to it. Don't hang about, Staples, we all need a bit of a livener before the karaoke . . .'

She was a petite gothy looking girl, with clunky framed glasses, a plain black dress, thick tights and insanely expensive-looking leather boots.

Steve was slightly flustered. 'Nice boots,' was his ludicrously ham-fisted opening gambit.

'What do you want?'

'Um, well . . . I, er . . .' She rolled her eyes.

'Coke's fifty, proper coke's eighty, three Es are a fiver, I've got mandy, k, acid – but I do NOT recommend that unless you've got Monday and Tuesday off – resin, skunk and some nice mild Thai grass.'

'Oh, right, could I have some coke please . . .' He had not felt more like a child in years.

'How much?'

'Sorry, I forgot, how much was it again?'

'Not the money, how many grams?'

'Oh, right, sorry!' he mumbled. 'Um . . . One?' It was definitely a question. He was not acquitting himself at all well in this exchange.

'Fifty or eighty?'

'Oh, yeah, right . . . Hang on . . .' he fumbled in his back pocket for his wallet. He felt his cheeks gently warming. He would make Taylor fucking pay for this. He opened the wallet and did the mental arithmetic in his head. He had bought the last round and was somewhat less flush than he had remembered. 'Just a fifty for now, please . . .' He felt like a child going to the sweet shop on their own for the first time, such was the odd mix of fear and excitement.

The woman rolled her eyes and reached inside the neck of her dress which afforded Steve the quickest glimpse of bright pink lace. She glanced up and caught him peeking and her eyes held his in their steely gaze.

'*Really?*' she said. And Steve's face bloomed in florid embarrassment. She shook her head laughing to herself. 'That'll be fifty please, Mister Heffner.' Steve didn't get the reference but she hadn't called him Staples so he thought he'd quit while he was ahead, thrust the money into her hand and in a smooth motion she passed him a tiny, breast-warmed sachet of white powder, and he made good his escape.

So Mike calling him Staples in a toilet cubicle was something of a low point during this particular rite of passage – offering a 'livener' to work colleagues for the very first time. And there he was inhaling the beery breath of the two men who had the keys to the kingdom.

As he leaned over and poured just over half of the packet onto the cistern he suddenly panicked. What if they wanted another one? Taylor was a greedy fuck, and he really only wanted to share with Jon, but Taylor had put him on to Katie so he owed him. He raked the powder into three clumsy slugs and proffered a rolled twenty to Taylor who, of course, took the biggest. Cunt. His head whipped back exuberantly. 'This is the fucking fifty, Staples, you cheapskate cunt! I thought you wanted to get on in this fucking game, you muppet.'

Steve's face reddened and once again Jon stepped in. 'Oh, fucking shut up, Mike, he's on about a tenth as much money as you, so this is equivalent to you buying a hit at five hundred. I thought you worked in finance, *you muppet . . .*'

They way Jon emphasised this final word was in a mocking tone. It was Taylor's most commonly used insult in the office and this was him being told that everybody knew it and to wind in his fucking neck. Steve felt his cheeks cooling and a warm glow of satisfaction ran through him. And with a fake skip in his step, he wandered back into the insane cacophony of 'High Notes Karaoke Lounge'.

Karaoke is for many the chance to strut about onstage like they are rock stars. Karaoke in a room where ninety per cent of the participants are on coke is one of the grimmest things in the world. Unworkable dance moves vie with unreachable notes combined with an insufferable confidence. As Steve looked at the stage he thought to himself, 'I'm gonna sing the fucking *shit* out of 'Wonderwall' . . .' And he really did.

As he leaned against the bar a procession of colleagues and strangers all came up to offer him drinks and slap him on the back. He looked over to a nearby cubicle to see his mentor Jon Phelps raising a champagne glass and winking. He really had sung the absolute shit out of 'Wonderwall'; he was a good-looking lad and had a solid Thames Corridor baritone that he very much felt completely outdid the nasal Mancunian drone of the original. He grinned and took a massive gulp of cold lager and was delighted to see over the shoulders of the swarm of well-wishers, Mike Taylor sulkily pulling his coat on to his shoulders and stomping out into Leadenhall Market. The tide had finally turned. And the best fucking thing of all was that not one of the people who came up to him had called him Staples. This called for a celebration.

There was just so much room in the cubicle with just him in it and he had plenty of elbow room to expertly carve the remaining crystals into one hefty, unbroken, glistening three-inch line. As he left the bathroom he felt like a king. The slaps still came down on to his shoulders. People offered to buy him drinks. That bird from the Dubai desk handed him her business card, on which in a smooth even hand was written 'Give me a call sometime. Deb x' He had quite simply never felt this good in his life.

He soaked up the adoration for another two hours as a procession of eager young men tried to outdo his Oasis busting turn. But they all crashed and burned. Jon came up clamped an arm round his shoulders and whispered in his ear, 'Unconventional play there, Stevie boy, but fucking classic.' This was music to Steve's buzzing ears . . .

'Cheers, Jon . . .'

'You play your cards right, in two months, you could

be doing Taylor's job.' As Jon said this, he turned to face Steve. No trace of guile in his face. This was real, he was being told that he was being lined up for Taylor's job. Part of him wanted to text Taylor right there and then. 'Be smart, Webb. Don't fuck it up.' Steve wanted to kiss him.

'Yeah, fucking A, Jon. I won't let you down, mate.'

'Good.'

'Er, where are you going?'

'Somewhere I'm going to take you once you've got Taylor's gig. Somewhere posh, classy and fucking expensive. Go home.'

'Alright, will do, Jon, seeya tomorrow . . .'

Most of the staff had left the bar to catch trains home, or snog or piss in City doorways. And the stragglers were still murdering the classics onstage. He turned to the bar and brandished a suspiciously curly twenty-pound note. 'Barkeep! A large JD please . . .' The surly Bulgarian barmaid bumped an optic twice, set the glass in front of Steve and took the money. Steve sipped the warming brown liquor, the usual burn of the spirits negated by the numbing alkaloid he had recently ingested.

The first thing he noticed when he heard the sound was that the hairs stood up on his arms and his cock began to swell. He set the glass down immediately. Was that a noise in the room or was it one he was just hearing in his head? As he turned to see the source of the sound, he realised that the bar was nearly empty now. And onstage, two girls were sharing the microphone and making the most extraordinary sound he had ever heard.

There weren't any words. It was just a simple repeated melody, which swirled around him. The notes ebbed and flowed. It was almost as if he could feel the notes fluttering into his ears individually and in pairs whenever the harmony demanded it.

He was sure he knew the song. It sounded like something from a long time ago. Maybe it was a Beatles album track, his dad was a huge Beatles fan and it was always on. Maybe he was remembering some distant once-heard melody from his childhood. He slowly walked towards the stage and the two women.

They were insanely beautiful, dark almond eyes and rivers of cascading auburn hair. And they looked eerily similar. Sisters? They surely must be sisters and they must have been singing together forever. It was fucking extraordinary. He stood in front as more of these pure arrows of sound entered him. Maybe it was the coke and the booze and the good news from Jon. Maybe any old shit would sound like the greatest song in the fucking world to him in this mind state. But as he watched them and listened to their singing he knew in his heart that it wasn't true. This was their doing. This pure, beautiful noise that was filling his ears and his soul was coming out of these two extraordinary women. He wandered closer to the stage, and noticed something about how they were singing. Their arms were always moving slowly about them, like sea grass in a current gently waving, but occasionally, they would touch each other and it was only when they were physically touching that they would sing together. As soon as the contact of skin on skin was broken one or other of them would continue the melody alone.

As he drew closer to the stage they looked down at him, and then he saw that they must be sisters, twins even. As their eyes met his, they held hands and the singing grew in intensity and he felt his cock harden and shifted his weight in front of them stooping clumsily. He was becoming intoxicated by this sensation. He should offer to buy them a drink. Fuck it. Break into his over-draft and use the plastic to get a bottle of bubbly. He simultaneously cursed that he was now out of cocaine. Looking up at them he wondered which of them he should have a tilt at. Maybe both. This day was going so fucking well, why not ride the streak? He opted for the direct approach.

'Buy you a drink, girls?'

They looked at him, smiling and just carried on sing-ing. He reiterated a little louder. 'Can I buy you a drink?'

They still did not respond but smiled at him and con-tinued the eerie harmony, their fingers intertwined with each other. Steve was becoming intoxicated with this, and briefly wondered if he might have been spiked at some point? Might Taylor in an act of indignation have slipped some Ketamine into his drink? But somehow he knew it wasn't that. He absolutely knew that it was the music doing this. The voices of these two sisters.

He retreated to the corner of the bar and they con-cluded their strange wordless melody with a crescendo of such soul scorching beauty that he found himself cry-ing with pure joy. They were the only people in the bar. No bar staff. No colleagues. He looked at his watch. It was 5 o'clock in the morning. 'Fuck sake, that's a fuck-ing Tissot, I only changed the battery a month ago and it's fucked!' He took his iPhone out and pressed the but-ton, 05.01 it read. He had lost six hours somewhere. He looked up at the stage and the sisters were gone. In front of him on the table was a small silver plate with a credit card receipt for three bottles of champagne. When the fuck had he bought three bottles of champagne at £175 a pop? He looked around the deserted bar for any sign of life but there was none. No staff, but more troublingly, no sisters.

He stepped out into Leadenhall Street and shouted, 'Hello? Ladies?' He looked left and right and just turning down an alley he saw the unmistakable figures of the two sisters and immediately broke into a sprint. Fuck, he was quite pissed, and was lurching from side to side, almost coming to grief over a kerb at one point. As he got to the corner they had turned down he felt he'd made good progress and now must have almost caught up. As he made the turn he could barely believe his eyes, they were a full two hundred metres further on. They had, if anything, stretched their lead on him. 'OY! GIRLS! WAIT! WHERE THE FUCK Y'GOING?' They turned into Fenchurch Street itself and he started running again, even faster. The streets were deserted, no paper vans, no milk floats, no stragglers cabs, no night buses. Nothing. But Steve didn't really notice this as he was too focused on catching up with the two women. As he leathered round the corner into Fenchurch Street again they were even further away, three hundred metres now, just about to turn into Fenchurch Street train station. His chest was burning with the effort and his feet hurt. He had to find these women. The pounding of his feet echoed down the concrete canyon of Fenchurch Street. His pace increased, he pushed his body harder and harder, these birds must be fucking athletes or something.

As he ran onto the station concourse it was 05.08 and there was no sign of the girls. The 05.10 was due to leave any minute. He vaulted the barriers and was gratified to see that there were no staff on duty. The 05.10 was comprised of eight carriages and juddered quietly.

Down at the far end of the train he saw the sisters boarding, 'OY!' he bellowed, as the hiss of the doors prompted him to leap onto the train. Now he had them. They wouldn't get away now. Nowhere to run. As the train drew out of Fenchurch Street station he began to work his way along the carriage. The tannoy announcement made him jump: 'This is the 05.10 direct service to Benfleet. The next stop will be Benfleet.' What? He had been travelling on the c2c all his life. There's no such service as a direct train to Benfleet. But he's never travelled that early in the morning so maybe he was wrong. Perhaps it was a special.

The train rumbled out of London through the low grey-green marshland of the Thames Estuary. Industry giving way to salty fields unsuitable for anything but the grazing of travellers' horses and the hardiest of sheep. Steve dropped off just east of Barking and awoke with a start upon hearing, 'The next stop is Benfleet. Passengers for Canvey Island please alight here.' Finally he'd find them. They were probably foreign anyway, maybe that's why they'd ignored him. Fucking mad athlete bitches. He'd get to the bottom of this. The waters of Benfleet Creek came into view and the train slowed down and he stood by the end door of the fourth carriage. As the train drew to a halt he pressed the door button and it hissed open; he left the train and turned right running for the front carriage where his mystery women awaited. But as he thundered up to the carriage he saw that it was empty. That was impossible. He had seen them board. The fucking thing hadn't stopped. He looked all around and shouted, 'HELLO!!!' His shout echoed down the platform and then he heard it. The singing.

He turned back down the train to see the two figures

step out of the carriage he had been in. That was simply not possible. The realisation that Fucking Mike Phelps had almost definitely spiked him briefly surfaced in his mind before dissolving in the beauty of the sound. They walked slowly out of the station and he followed. But he did not run. Every time he ran he ended up further away.

He kept to their pace. It was counter intuitive, sure, but maybe if he didn't run he might get closer. This thought sort of slowly dissolved in his mind as the pure soaring beauty of the sound of the women entered him once more. They were fifty yards away and it sounded utterly amazing. He didn't believe that anything could sound so beautiful. The tears rolled down his face as the purity of sound began to unmake him from within.

They turned off the Benfleet Road east towards the Creek and Leigh-on-Sea and the path to Two Tree Island. He slowly kept pace with their steps but was happy to be anywhere that he could hear them. Random notions swam through him. He'd quit his job and just follow these women. He knew that is all he would need. To live within the sound that had now completely enveloped him. He realised that the joy he had felt earlier at his successes, at his petty victories, was utterly meaningless. The only thing that was important was the sound. Was the singing. Was their voices. His life finally had a real purpose.

At the end of the path he expected to emerge and see them just ahead along the sea wall. But again they had vanished. His heart began to ache with the thought of losing them. The most all-encompassing sorrow began to surge through him. But then . . . like a miracle he heard them once more. He looked all around. Where could they be? The sound was so pure and so clear. They must be close. He turned to his right and saw them standing hand in hand on the north edge of Canvey at the side of Benfleet Creek. How had they crossed the water? The bridge was a quarter of a mile back past the marina. It was impossible.

But so what if it was impossible. They still sang so everything was alright. The sisters' hands gripped each other and they extended their arms towards him. There would be no more running. No getting away. They were finally going to wait for him. The bridge was too far away and he didn't want to lose them. He smiled at them, the tears now running down his face. The pure beauty of the moment owned him completely. He stepped towards the creek. His feet at first making shallow slimy prints in the slick grey mud. Then with each advancing step towards the unbelievable sound they sank a little deeper. His next step was into the chill Thames water of the creek. A second step into the creek and he was up to the middle of his thighs now. The water was icy cold but felt pure and clear to him, like the pure clarity of his thoughts. He must just get to the other side of this stretch of water and everything would be fine. He would be whole. He would have meaning. He would be loved.

He was up to his waist and looked up at the beautiful faces of the women. He shivered with the cold and took another step. He had reached the actual channel and sunk a full foot deeper. He was up to his shoulders. Marching forward towards his dream, towards completion. Towards life and light and love. But a thought, a single thought was fluttering somewhere, 'Steve! Excuse me! Steve!' Oh, go away you silly thought. I'm going to be happy now. Beneath the water he took another step towards his goal. But that pesky thought was really shouting quite loudly now, 'Steve! Steve! STEVE! STEPHEN!!!!' His next step was into deep water and did not find the bottom and his head slipped below the surface and his mouth filled with the salt silty ice cold waters of the Thames.

And at that moment he was awake. And at that moment he realised where he was. And at that moment he realised he was going to die very soon. And at that moment as his head broke the surface briefly before sinking forever he heard the words to the haunting melody that had summoned him to this being sung by the two dark-eyed women.

Dear Stephen
Sweet Stephen
Stephen of our hearts
So sad to say
So sad to know
That you, my love
Cannot swim . . .

MICHAEL LEGGE

THE DREAM OF NIGHTMARES

'DIBS MCCAWE WAS killed by her lover, not her husband, and he buried her in a shallow grave near their love nest because he thought she was having an affair and he was lazy.'

Gwen couldn't sleep. She couldn't ever sleep. Her bed was broken, with the frame of it vaguely held in place by five old VHS cassettes stacked underneath it; her bedroom was cold and her husband kept saying the stupidest things in his sleep. Every night.

She sat up in bed for hours, again, and just stared. Alf would have no idea in the morning because Gwen would never tell him. He just assumed that she was always tired because she worked so hard on her special projects. The whole house was always spotless because she kept it that way, she kept fit by keeping fit and she gave back to the community by volunteering to assist at a local petting zoo. Of course really she had a cleaner in to tidy, instead of breakfast and lunch she smoked and she visited the petting zoo simply because goats rarely judged if you spent all day smoking and weeping. That was Gwen's real life; pretending that everything was OK while she tried to figure out why she hadn't gone mad yet. Or if she had gone mad years ago. Either way, throwing days away and telling people she was busy seemed to be the easiest way to deal with life just for now. And at the end of the day she would cook a beautiful meal for her husband (get a takeaway) and then treat herself to a good night's sleep (stay up all night listening to him talking shit).

It was an unbearable situation but it gave Gwen a wonderful chance to pretend to be patient. In real life, she had no patience whatsoever but being with Alf seemed so like something Stephen King would make up and publish under a pseudonym that she decided to just pretend to be a different person almost all the time. In this pretend life Gwen had friends that she liked, a husband who wasn't a dickhead, a working bed and a heart of gold. Only two months ago, Alf had been in a coma after an industrial accident at his life drawing class. For those two months Gwen visited him every few days in hospital, held his hand and pretended to support him. She would bring him grapes; read the first few paragraphs of a book to him; eat his grapes. She was the perfect wife. It was during her third phone conversation with her solicitor about the sale of their house that Alf opened his eyes.

Gwen pretended that Alf's open eyes were a blessing just as she was pretending that his closed eyes right now weren't making her want to tear her own head off and club him to death with it. Other partners snored, hers talked arse.

'The missing money is distributed to seven different accounts,' he would say. Or, 'She's still alive. Check the ice cream van' or, 'It was suicide. He made it look like murder. He likes attention.' Well, it was just another one of those awful nights. A night when he slept and talked nuts and she finally went downstairs to watch TV that even she couldn't pretend was good.

Good or bad, the blue-green glow of the television is the true friend of the insomniac and just what Gwen needed right now. In the warmth of cold entertainment, Gwen could be herself. Mumbling, sniffing and smoking out the window. She was finally her. She didn't feel the need to showbusinessly sing *I Am What I Am* but it felt good to just not be smiling or saying nice things or taking an interest in an anecdote that made her teeth die of boredom. Why did she worry so much about how people saw her? Why did she care if people thought she wasn't perfect? Why was she so afraid to face life and just be herself? I've no idea. Probably the same reason you do it. Gwen got through six cigarettes, two episodes of a behated sitcom, half a chat show and then went back to a spot of slight pretending. She put the news on. She wasn't pretending that she wanted to take an interest in current affairs, she was just pretending that she had an interest in current affairs. If only there was a way of knowing things without finding out about them, she thought. Then the newsreader said something familiar.

'Missing student Becky Willoughby has been found alive after a twenty-three-day hunt by the Metropolitan Police. A man has been taken into custody. The missing student was found handcuffed and blindfolded in an ice cream van thought to be owned by a neighbour . . .'

Gwen lit another cigarette and thought, I could have

told you that. She sucked in the beautiful chemicals and breathed out the romantic smoke. Then for the next forty seconds she tried to choke as quietly as possible while pointing at the television in disbelief.

No. No, no, no, no, no, no, no. That cannot have happened. The news cannot have just reported a thing Alf said because that's not how the news works and the things Alf says are just the words of a nutcase dreaming and it must be a coincidence and that is frightening and there is no way that this has happened. Alf can't be involved in a kidnapping.

Actually, that's true. Alf really couldn't be involved in a kidnapping. He hasn't the time. And he's an idiot. He didn't used to be, he was OK once. Had ideas, wore decent shoes. But since the accident he's just been all about work and talking in his sleep. He realised that life is too short and he has to live it and he talks in his sleep. He said all he wants to do is look after Gwen and make sure she's happy. He said that while he was awake, by the way. He sleeps beside Gwen, goes to work and then comes home again to sleep beside her. And he definitely goes to work. She's gone with him enough times. And he gets a paycheck. And he messages her all day from the office email to see if she's alright or if she needs anything. I mean, he *could* use the office email when he's out of the office and being a criminal but . . . Alf just wouldn't know how to do that. He didn't know how to retweet never mind hide an entire woman in an ice cream van while pretending to have a job. He just works, sleeps and then talks. And the madness he comes out with while asleep is just babbling. Dark, crime-obsessed babbling. Gwen switched on her laptop to look up some of the other insane jabber that her husband came out with. It's not like anything else Alf spoke about in his sleep would turn out to solve an actual real crime. Gwen LOL'd (i.e. she made no noise at all). Funny if it did though.

No. It would be terrifying.

Gwen paced the living room floor pretending unconvincingly that she wasn't going to throw up. The 'killer used his brother's shovel' story from three months ago was there on the BBC news website. So was the 'there was no twin. He did it all himself' robbery and the 'it was no accident, he knew the chainsaw was a go-er' trial. Everything Alf had said was there. All those crimes he predicted in his sleep and here they were solved, often too late. Gwen circled the room again, went back to her laptop and unfashionably Yahooed the name 'Dibs McCawe'. And that's when the truth came out.

Gwen threw up on her own leg.

Dibs McCawe was missing. MISSING. Not dead.

For months – oh, stop pretending – for years Gwen had been wondering what she was supposed to do in life and now she realised her purpose. She could save a life. Alf had a gift. Maybe. An incredible gift that could change the world. Through Alf, there could be a world without crime. No murder, no violence, no fear. To change the entire world, all she needed to do was listen to Alf talk in his sleep and then tell him to inform the police. Or . . . she could just say that she'd worked it out herself.

Gwen didn't need to spend her days crying in a petting zoo necessarily. She could be a master sleuth.

Gwen tied her long blonde hair (dyed) into a bunch and sat cross-legged in front of her laptop. The news of Dibs's disappearance was everywhere on the internet. Every detail of a real life accessible to anyone who noticed if they clicked on it. Her parents' names, her hometown, her school, her workplace, her best friend, her hobbies, her husband's name, his work associate . . . Would it be too corny if the work associate was also Dibs McCawe's lover? No. This pretend detective knew exactly what she was probably doing.

What she was probably doing was nuts. Even she knew that. But she hadn't slept in days and going to the London offices of DeHolt, the highly questionable pharmaceutical company where Trent McCawe and his associate Peter Knox worked, to do some spying seemed utterly reasonable. Gwen could pretend to enjoy making Alf his breakfast another time, he'd have to make it himself. She wanted to get to the DeHolt building before anyone else. Three hours before anyone else.

Less than an hour into her new detective job and Gwen had come to the conclusion that it was mainly boring. She liked the hat she'd picked out for herself that morning but, other than that, being a detective was mainly just waiting. So far it had been two hours of standing in the rain, staring at an empty office building and looking great in a frankly fabulous hat. Even when people started arriving for work, she didn't really know what to do. She was good at stopping them and saying, 'Excuse me, I'm a detective' but after that it all went downhill. What was a detective supposed to ask people? 'Was Dibs McCawe nice?' seemed irrelevant, not to mention stupid. And 'Do you have Peter Knox's home address?' might give the game away and was creepy. Gwen didn't want anyone thinking her pretend detective was really stupid or really weird so instead, after much thought, she decided to just stand in the rain and wait again. Maybe by the time they all come out she'll have thought of something to ask them. Still, lovely hat.

The great thing about starting something that makes you feel stupid is that you don't eventually feel stupid about it. Feeling stupid was there from the beginning. But even Gwen had to admit that standing outside a building from 6 a.m. to 2.45 p.m. just to get rained on seemed stupider than she anticipated. It was nice to smoke and cry somewhere new but, as far as finding Dibs McCawe alive and well went, it all looked pointless. Gwen thought about all the detective books she'd started to read over the years. How did Inspector Morse, John Rebus have the patience for this? Just when she finally decided to give up and go home for the fifth time, a black cab pulled up outside DeHolt. A man got out and said 'I'll be five minutes' to the cab driver. It was Peter Knox. He was a tall, dark-haired handsome man in his late thirties. Not Johnny Depp handsome but definitely handsome. Like if they needed someone to play Roger Moore in a film about the making of *The Wild Geese*, they'd get Peter Knox. And there he was. Right in front of Gwen. He entered DeHolt and Gwen knew she had five minutes. Now what?

The only idea she had was to scream 'He kidnapped Dibs McCawe!' over and over again as he came out of the building. It was a brilliant idea with just one flaw: it was a rubbish idea. He'd jump in the cab, get to his house and Gwen's excitement at being a detective would just speed up Dibs's eventual murder. She was out of her depth, she was relying on evidence her husband mumbled in his sleep and she was panicking. She wasn't a detective. She wasn't saving someone's life. She was nothing.

Knox left the building, got into the cab and it drove off. Gwen turned away and felt useless. She could go to the police, of course. She could tell them that her husband had a dream about how Dibs McCawe would eventually be found. They'd pretend to take her details and they'd swear blind they'd follow the lead up. The poor woman, thought Gwen. She hailed a cab. She just wanted to be home where it was warm and dry and false.

'Where to, Miss?' asked the cab driver. Looking through the windscreen, Gwen could see Peter Knox's car in front of her, driving away with her new dream and all she wanted to say was 'home'. Then her eyes widened and the most exciting thing that ever happened to Gwen in her entire life just burst out of her mouth, 'Follow that cab.'

The cab driver put his foot down hard on the accelerator, sending the cab speeding forwards and Gwen flying backwards into her seat. 'Please,' she shouted with a thrill. Even when you're an adventurous detective hunting down a man in a case that could mean life or death, there's no need for bad manners.

The cabs zigzagged through the frustration of London traffic to the extravagant home of Peter Knox. As his cab pulled into the driveway, Gwen asked her cab driver to stop. She got out, paid the fare and went back to waiting. His cab left and she heard the front door of his house close. It was time to snoop, if that was the correct technical term.

You didn't need to be a brand new detective to spot that Peter Knox's house was huge. Gwen crept around the outside, peered through windows, hid behind pillars and sighed at lovely plants; God, his house was flipping

gorgeous. If Dibs McCawe really was being held cap-
tive here then Gwen hated her for it. The lucky cow. She
hunched by a window at the side of the house. There
was no one there; just a running machine, a cross-train-
er, a Swiss ball . . . Aw, he has a gym in his house. Gwen
would love a gym. She'd never use it but no one would
ever know that. The room had so many sets of weights.
Enough for a Russian weightlifter or Dolph Lundgren in
one of the Rockys. But not Peter Knox. He's just not that
big. Not even close.

Near the back of the huge house was another huge
building. It looked like a garage but only if your car was
a Concorde. The main front doors of the building were
locked so Gwen crept along the side and peered through
the windows.

Cars. There must have been fifteen of them. All looking beautifully brand new and shiny, even the old ones.
Sleek red Ferrari sat next to luxurious Rolls-Royces that
sat next to what Gwen could only assume were Chitty Chitty Bang Bangs. If she had cars like these, Gwen
thought, no way would she ever take a cab. Although
Gwen couldn't drive so she'd actually have no choice
. . . wait a minute; why would a man who can't drive
want to own a series of classic cars? And what cars
they were. Gwen looked in through the windows at
Jaguars, Maseratis, Dibs McCawe, Aston Martins and
shit, shit, shit, shit, shit Dibs McCawe is in there. She's
in there and she's tied to a chair and she's gagged and
she's looking at Gwen and she's trying to scream and
Gwen is panicking and Gwen doesn't want to be there
anymore.

This was too easy. Two minutes of snooping and
she'd found the missing woman. She called the police

and told them she'd found Dibs. After hanging up, Gwen looked in at Dibs and tried to make a face that suggested the police were on their way so just relax. A sort of smile, eyebrows raised, head wobble thing. Then she just stood there in the rain and waited with Dibs. Standing in a beautiful but soaking wet garden while a criminal was probably in his Jacuzzi or his billiard room completely unaware that his evil plot had been foiled really easily.

Less than ten minutes went by and sirens blazed as police cars skidded to a halt outside Peter Knox's house. Peter burst out of the frankly beautiful doors at the back of his house and ran to the rear of his garden.

'Excuse me,' Gwen called to the police. 'He's just here if you want him.'

Peter Knox was handcuffed and led to a police car while Dibs McCawe was released and helped to an ambulance. Gwen stood beaming with pride as she was thanked and congratulated by every police officer who passed her. Detective Inspector Billingham was in charge of the case and just wanted to know how she figured out where Dibs was.

'Easy,' she said. 'You and I both know, Inspector, that Mr and Mrs McCawe weren't getting on but that's no reason to get rid of someone, is it? A career man like Mr McCawe doesn't want to go to jail, does he? So I gambled: why are they not getting on, I thought? Maybe she's having an affair. With his friend. It does happen. And look at him, he's addicted to success. He wants to have everything, even if he doesn't need it. House, cars, Swiss ball. And Mrs McCawe. I'm betting she wanted to call the affair off and he couldn't handle it. Bit too much like real life for him.'

Billingham was impressed, thanked Gwen for

her hard work and made it clear that if she ever tried anything like this again, he'd arrest her on a trumped-up charge of his choosing.

Sadly, Billingham hadn't a hope of that ever happening. Gwen was a hero. She was interviewed by the BBC, the *Guardian*, *Newsweek* and Graham Norton. She was everywhere. And it felt like every week she was solving another case: the Sedgwick murders, the Marchmonte robbery, the idiot embezzling mayor of old London Town. She solved them all. Not just the big crimes, she knew when kids were going to nick from newsagents too. She was given the Citizen of the Year Award from the Prime Minister herself. And she was loved. The nation adored that lovely lady with the incredible powers of deduction and snappy headwear. Gwen was everyone's hero.

Well, not everyone's. Some criminals hated her. She got threats. People setting up Twitter accounts just to tweet 'Stop now or you'll die :(' to her before quickly deleting their account. She got phone calls. Not many. But enough 'You're dead' phone calls to make it uncomfortable. And Detective Inspector Billingham wasn't keen on her either. She'd been making him and the rest of the police look like fools. And how?

How? It was all down to Alf. Dependable Alf. A man who realised that, after an accident at work, he might not be here forever and he must do everything to provide for Gwen while he still can. He didn't take time off after the accident. He came out of a coma and went straight back to work. Every day. Long hours. He had a responsibility. He had to face that responsibility. He loved Gwen and couldn't bear to think of her unhappy. And look at her now. A master detective with a skill that he could never understand. If only he knew. After the accident, Alf had contracted a rare cerebral condition that let his mind predict the future and only Gwen knew about it and understood it. (This is a short story, reader. Google it.)

Billingham had a few more questions to ask about the arrest of Frazer Tuckley. How did Gwen know that Tuckley had even planned to rob the Eurostar? 'Well, he was very quiet,' said Gwen. 'That's always suspicious.'

Sure enough, guns were found at Tuckley's flat along with blueprints of trains and tunnels. It certainly seemed that Gwen was right. The BBC wanted an interview with Gwen outside the station and as Tuckley and his men were led inside they screamed threats. 'You're dead.' Words Gwen had heard before and shrugged off. But sitting in his work canteen watching TV was Alf. All he had felt about Gwen's new life was pride but this is not how he saw heroes being treated. No one shouted 'You're dead' at Ace Ventura or The Hulk.

The Hulk isn't real though. Gwen is. And so are dangerous men.

Alf didn't sleep a wink that night.

Gwen woke up with a start. She was startled by both her phone ringing and by how she had clearly had a proper good night's sleep. That hadn't happened in months. It was Billingham and he sounded serious. Not just serious but sad. He needed Gwen's help. God, he hated that. Just asking for it left a bad taste in his mouth, like he'd just brushed his teeth and then had a Lucozade and then was sick. Gwen joyously rushed to the station. She was famous but she was still humble enough to let the police beg her for help.

Billingham was completely certain that Gwen knew about the two North London drownings even though she had never heard of them. With TV, radio and podcast interviews, Gwen hadn't the time to keep abreast of the very thing she was pretending to be an expert in. He hated admitting it but the award-winning Gwen was the only person he knew that might have a hope of solving the case quickly. And if she didn't? Even better. Two women had been killed. It was obviously someone hoping to become a serial killer one day but why, how and who? It made Billingham sick to the stomach of his guts and yet Gwen assured him that she understood the details and would crack the case quicker than a policeman getting to his third hallo.

Alf lay deeply awake. It was his second night without sleep. Every time he closed his eyes he saw Frazer Tuckley's face and heard 'You're dead' constantly screaming in his head. Gwen got into bed beside him, said 'Goodnight' and waited for Alf to sleep. This case was important and she needed to crack it to keep her reputation solid and, you know, to save any other people from being killed. But Alf didn't sleep. He just lay there, wide awake with fear.

'How long do you think you'll do this crime solving thing then?' asked Alf.

Oh, no. Alf was talking. Alf never goes to bed and talks. Not while he's awake anyway. He works so hard that he's normally asleep before he gets into bed so why is he talking? Gwen knew he was concerned for her so she gave him the answer she thought he wanted to hear, the one that wasn't true. 'Oh, not long,' she said. 'I'm getting bored of it anyway.' There. That sounded right. A little lie to help give Alf some piece of mind and to get him to go to bloody sleep. This was the only chance that Gwen had to stop this killer and to secure her status as the country's number one pretend detective. All she needed was for Alf to go to sleep.

The sun beamed through the curtains and woke Gwen up. 'Aw, shit.'

She got dressed and hopped downstairs at the same time to find Alf ready for work and looking exhausted. 'Erm . . . Are you alright?' she said. 'I mean . . . Good morning.'

'Couldn't sleep again,' Alf replied, then kissed her and left for work.

No. No, Alf had to sleep. Gwen was famous now and she liked it and everyone liked her and her lovely hat was in all the papers and Alf HAD TO SLEEP. How could she face everyone she'd lied to if Alf won't sleep?

Billingham rang. He had some new information. A list of suspects, men that both women knew on a social networking site. Is there more than one killer? Did these women ever actually meet this man or men? Is this even the right lead to follow? Gwen didn't know. Of course she didn't know. All this sleep made it hard to think. She agreed that this was all good information and she'd look into it and she hadn't a clue what she was talking about. She pretended her phone went dead by hanging up and then she pretended she didn't have a phone by putting it in a drawer. Snap out of it, Gwen. You're an award-winning detective. You can do this. A bit.

Gwen spent the day reading about the two recently killed women. So much information and she understood none of it. She read a long article on the *Daily Mail* website about how the police were baffled by the case and how tragic the murders were and about how the women were both good, decent, non-immigrant people. Then, at the very bottom of the comments section, Gwen saw her future. 'Where is Gwen when we need her?' wrote a reader who was known for their very racist comments on other 'stories'. And that racist was right. Where is Gwen? Well, she could lie here on the floor feeling sick all day or she could finally face the truth and actually do something to make all this right. Gwen put on her coat, went out and bought a load of sleeping pills.

When Alf got home that night, Gwen had dinner all ready for him. She'd cooked (well, bought) his favourite. Curry, onion bhajis, coconut rice and a load of crushed up sleeping pills. 'Something smells great,' said Alf as soon as he walked in the door and stepped over the post. Gwen always ignored the post and, as always, Alf picked it up and looked through it. Bills, junk and a brown envelope with no stamp, no name and no address. Gwen served the meal while Alf opened the envelope. Inside was a single A4 sheet of paper with 'You're Dead' written on it.

'Dinner time!' she said with a smile. Alf walked into the kitchen and handed the paper to Gwen. 'I don't think I'm hungry,' he said.

It was just someone trying to scare her, Gwen explained. A crazy fan, an idiot. Someone who was jealous. It's not from Frazer Tuckley. He's in prison. And it's not from one of his henchmen. No, she was sure it wasn't from one of them. It's just an idiot. She had the full support of the Metropolitan Police force behind her. Who would really threaten her knowing that? Now, eat up. It's nothing. Eat up. She wasn't bothered by a silly old death threat and neither should he. Now, really. Eat up.

Alf couldn't face food. Gwen looked at him and

she could see he loved her. Alf could provide for her but he couldn't protect her. Not from a crazed murderer anyway. Gwen knew that Alf wanted all this to stop and for them to return to a normal life so that she was safe, secure and always loved. And Gwen began to cry.

She always got her way when she cried and Alf wolfed down the meal in minutes. 'That was delicious,' he said with his mouth full. 'Good,' said Gwen. 'Maybe we'll have an early night?'

It was 7.10 p.m. and Alf was fast asleep in bed. Gwen got her notepad and pen ready, indispensable tools for any detective. Especially pretend ones with husbands that solve crimes in their sleep. She sat beside him on the bed and waited.

Alf was right, of course. This was dangerous. But it was exciting too. Not the lying in bed waiting for Alf to start sleep talking bit, but the other bits. The being on TV bits and being written about in the paper. People recognising her in the street and getting an award and the fan mail. Not the 'You're dead' fan mail but the nice 'You're the best' and 'I love your hat' messages she got on Twitter. But Alf was right. This had to stop. One day.

Gwen picked up her Citizen of the Year award from the bedside table and looked at it proudly, at first, and then ashamed. It didn't belong to her. She'd stolen Alf's gift to make her feel better about herself and awards mean nothing if you haven't earned them. The award looked like a small Cleopatra's Needle: made of glass and very, very shiny. So shiny that Gwen could see her reflection in it and that's when she put it on the floor, out of sight. Sometimes even Gwen couldn't stand the sight of Gwen.

Maybe it really was time to admit the truth. Well, not admit it. She just had to stop pretending. Lying.

Then Alf spoke.

Gwen spun round, grabbed her notepad and pen and accidentally kicked her Citizen of the Year award sending it smashing into three bits. 'She died,' said Alf. No time to care about the award now and anyway there'll be plenty more awards were that came from if – WHEN – she solves this case. Alf continued to mumble.

'She died.'

Gwen tried to be patient. OK, Alf, we got that bit. Who died? Who? And how? And how do we stop her from dying?

'She died.'

Gwen started to pretend to stab him with her pen. Come on, Alf. Out with it.

'She was killed. Killed . . .'

Right.

'Gwen.'

She dropped her notepad and leapt across the room, cutting her foot on the broken glass on the floor. It was a small cut but enough to explain the feeling of blood draining from her face. Gwen's heart pounded with fear. No, he didn't just say her name. Tuckley's in prison. Everyone's in prison. He can't have said her name.

'Gwen.'

No.

'She was killed. Gwen killed. Gwen was killed.'

Gwen knew three other Gwens. There were probably more. It'll be another Gwen. Some other Gwen that deserved a good murdering. It can't be her.

'Gwen the detective.'

Great.

'She was killed. Gwen killed. Poison.'

Poison?

'Poison. Gwen. The killer . . . The killer . . . The killer in the house.'

Gwen screamed. Tuckley's escaped. Knox has escaped. Every single person in prison had escaped and they've hunted her down. They've hunted her down and they'll make her pay for her lies. Gwen threw up. It helped her think.

'Gwen. Poison. Killer in the house.'

Alf. She needed Alf. Gwen ran to her sleeping husband and shook him. He reacted like any overweight, middle-aged, life-size rag doll. 'Wake up,' she threatened while repeatedly slapping his face. Nothing. Alf just lay there, peacefully drugged. 'Wake up,' she screamed again. Every noise in the house was a potential killer. Was that just a breeze making the tree branch lightly tap the window or was it Frazer Tuckley thumping up the stairs with a high-calibre assault axe? That sounded like the boiler switching off but it also sounded exactly like Peter Knox laughing insanely while revving up a chainsaw. 'Wake the fuck up.' But all she got was Alf sleeping soundly and mumbling, 'Killer in the house.'

'I'll stop,' Gwen negotiated. 'I'll stop right now. No more detective, Alf. You were right. I was wrong. Now, please wake up.'

'Killer in the house.'

If there really was a killer in the house then Gwen had no choice. She needed to get out. No. HE needed to get her out. This was all Alf's fault anyway. Sort of. There's no choice. Alf had to wake up or they'll both die.

'Killer in the house.'

'I'm well aware of that, thanks Alf,' said Gwen as

she grabbed him by the pyjama collar and dragged him to the edge of the bed. If he stood up, he'd wake up, she reasoned. She wrapped her arms around his waist and pulled him close to her, face to face. He was easily twice her weight but she had to try.

'Killer in the house.'

'Help me, Alf,' she said, took a deep breath and lifted her deadweight husband to his lifeless feet. He reminded her that the killer was in the house one more time before she told him to shut up and shuffled his useless body just inches before he slouched forward and took Gwen with him. She hit the floor and felt the thud of the floorboards on her skull and the sharp, shattered base of the Citizen of the Year award piercing into her back. She opened her eyes just in time to see the lifeless Alf come crashing down on top of her.

As his weight hit her, the award tore through the flesh of her back, between her ribs and directly stabbing into her right lung.

She couldn't breathe and, with Alf on her chest and throat, she couldn't even scream out the pain that was within. She lay there, trapped and suffocating, with the man who loved her on top mumbling.

'Poisoned food with sleeping pills. Tried to warn her. The killer was in the house. The killer was in the house.'

NEIL EDMOND

ALL WARM INSIDE

HE WOKE, SATISFIED, crouching in darkness. He wasn't sure he'd slept. If that had been sleep, he barely felt refreshed. More smug. A job well done.

His brain fumbled casually with the absence of duvet and mattress and pillow, the musty scent of pine obscuring something rich and human, the lack of elbow room . . . but then set them aside and suggested he extend his woolly reverie with a fondle. It was too cramped, too close to masturbate, though he tried, stretching an arm awkwardly beneath his thigh to cup his balls, which shied away, back into his interior. Perhaps they knew something he didn't.

His fingers stank. He felt mainly naked. One sock, perhaps, unless that foot was numb. There was wood beneath the other, and at his back and shoulder. His eyes swam in blackness, unable to settle on anything but their own grainy splashes of effort. This was not a happy place, he realised. His pride congealed into unease and slid into his stomach which puckered and cooled – he had a sudden sense of having rummaged inside a man, tugging bowels from sac, briefly wearing them, a ruddy parade – then he shuddered violently and something touched his shoulder.

He stood, flailed and span endlessly, snagged in tendrils, shouting fucks and clouting wood and then – through a sudden yawn of light – he toppled backwards.

He lay on carpet, panting at an open wardrobe.

Were they his clothes, dancing on their hangers, rattling at him? A fraying shirt, pale jeans, a cardigan? Was that his style? He couldn't say. He didn't know.

Light, from a red-flecked strip above his head, demanded identity, so he looked at his hands. They were crusted with red and brown and strings of meat, and ached now they'd been seen. His nails were ragged, but he didn't fancy chewing them, not yet. He peered further, past his reluctant genitals, to his foot. 'It *was* a sock,' he mentioned, and his voice sounded as he thought it should: a man's, relieved, parched, a little short of breath. The sock was less familiar, sopped in gore. And striped.

A stuffiness, a Guinness tang, a hum of piss, the buzz of flies left little doubt. Something bad had happened here. With a sulking reluctance, he sat up and faced the room.

It was small and square and spattered with man. A central mass of person, ruined, lay a few feet to his right, then spiralled out about the place, in splashes and clumps of flesh and little mounds of organ. On a small single bed a rope of viscera had been milked for stools, which lolled reeking on a pillow. 'I'm sorry,' he said, feeling implicated. He considered returning to the wardrobe, but no.

He retched. A dribble of spit did nothing to counter

his discomfort. With a little effort, adjusted to all fours, back arched, head down, he managed to produce a puddle of froth. Amid it was an eye. It was hazel brown, unseeing and unchewed, which seemed either gluttonous or overkeen or possibly accidental. He patted his own sockets, just in case, then opted to check the corpse.

It wore, or rather lay among, a suit. On the lapel was a name badge: Phil. If anything, the opposite had been done. Phil had been emptied, a great gash running from neck to navel, from which he spilled into the room so thoroughly. Limbs had been extruded beyond the confines of his clothing. Hands stamped flat, a knee kicked loose, the shin and foot torn from the trouser leg and propped against a chair, still socked and shod. A tatty rupture gashed the calf where the fib – or tib? – had been wrenched free. The sock was striped, Phil's other foot was bare and – oh, a shard of memory – he'd nicked that sock and popped it on while Phil lay warm and sputtering nearby – a punt at empathy, he hoped, companionship. At worst a form of flattery.

He found the tib – or fib – at the other end of Phil, jammed in his head via an eyehole, more spear than spoon, jarringly white above the mashed, purpling visage. In half-arsed symmetry a biro pierced the other eye, nib uppermost, lid free. He winced. More artfully, a spider plant had been patted into the gaping mouth, though the jaw was too limply piecemeal to offer much purchase and the skinny leaves straggled chestwards, an elven goatee. The work of a madman. Not him.

He should do the decent thing, but couldn't quite remember what that was. He found the pen lid near a flap of liver and tapped it back atop the pen, pulled the mattress from its frame and dragged it up to cover the excavated man, but stopped. Did he know him? He squinted at the battered face, blurring the insertions and distortions, and held it in his mind while rifling through a mental Rolodex which seemed to have been scorched with guilt or shame or – ah, a memory, his face, in here, unmashed, wide-eyed, agape, trying to say a thing, but – oh, just that. That and the name badge, 'Phil'.

He envied Phil his name. He had one himself, surely? There were things people called him, of course. 'Loser', 'twat' and 'nerk' – they pierced the fug that sat thickly on his sense of self, thicker than the stink of outed innards. 'My face,' he thought, 'I'll try my own,' and looked out for a mirror.

Beneath the crimson scattered layer of Phil, the room was bland, like some he'd seen on low-grade work trips, when he had worked at whatever he'd once done. Wardrobe, bed, desk, chair, no mirror, no telly, no kettle, no window, a door. A door.

He spent minutes kicking at the door, twisting at the sticky handle, denting it and clawing at the frame. This violence felt familiar and correct, though ineffective. He was locked in, which struck him as unfair. There was no en suite, which might excuse the urine pooled around Phil's face. 'I was watering the plant,' he mitigated, weakly, then, in sudden furious defiance, growled 'Hung for a sheep . . .' and shat into a corner. He wiped himself on a pair of blood-stained pyjamas that, too late – another shard – he realised were his.

He balked. He glanced back to the wardrobe. He'd hung his jeans on hangers, his shirts were tatty-cuffed, but clean. He may have wiped new stripes on to his jimjams, but he couldn't have done these other things, this bloody, murderous mess. At last, he felt clear-headed, a rush of certainty, responsibility, and took the opportunity to think.

He stood, one sock short of naked, breathed deeply and began. He would attempt to be forensic, standing like the redhead on a TV show he'd watched because a woman he liked had liked it. No, no good. The posture felt empty, unconvincing, not enough. He hated mysteries, twists, red herrings, cul-de-sacs, untruths. Give him the facts, the murderer up front, like – oh, at last – a larger piece of him was going to poke through all this fudge. He raised his fists toward the ceiling, waiting for his identity to crash back into him with a thunderbolt. 'COLUMBO!' he bellowed, and waited. But, no, that was it, an old man's name, not his. The memory guttered out of him with a growl. 'Just one more thing.'

He scuffed about through matted carpet, nudging grim bits with his toes. It seemed, perhaps, this was his fault. If so, he hadn't been himself. He'd seen such ugliness before, on sleepless sofa nights, unfolding on his meagre screen. Reason flooded him.

He checked his body for bites, signs of contagion. He sniffed and peeked beneath the door for a whiff of glowing mist. His flesh, where clean, was pink and lively. He wasn't craving brains. There was just one dead man in the room and it was not him.

He ran his tongue along his teeth, top and bottom. He found no fangs, though the ridges felt unfamiliar, cracked and coarsened. Phil had been chewed and ravaged by tooth and nail. No full moon in here, though, and those pyjamas had been discarded intact, not torn free in transformation. They had been worn, so he'd not been born from Phil full-sized, nor burst out of his chest, a rubber puppet. He scoured for signs of ritual: no pentacles, candles, or bloody scrawls. No book of human skin, no Japanese videotape, no puzzle box.

Frantically, he rolled his eyes back into his skull and looked for something squatting on his soul. He lumbered blindly about the room, backed into a corner, bent his limbs beyond their wishes and tried to levitate, crawl backwards up the wall. He slagged off God and priests and their mothers, but without conviction and the voice remained his own. His ankles hurt and he never left the ground.

What, then? He felt his back for switches, strafed his scalp for wires and antennae, for hints of remote control. He tore off his borrowed sock to reveal his hidden serial number, which was not there. Finally, with a shrug, he bent himself over the small desk and pushed a thumb and forefinger into his anus. 'Batteries?' he muttered glumly, but there were none. He was, as he'd feared, human.

If this was done by him, as him, a human man, he would have had good reason. There was a bed. Was this a sexual encounter gone awry? 'Am I a prostitute?' he mused. 'Was Phil a John gone wrong?' But the name badge, suit and room suggested 'conference', the pyjamas, even clean, said 'practical' and 'modest' not 'do me now'. He felt no enmity towards the corpse, he hadn't been provoked. There was just a sneaking sense of having done what was expected. An act of obedience, out of his hands. This must be his job.

He felt just like a soldier, or what he felt they must feel like. Righteous, confident, by any means necessary. But could those means include snapped ribs arrayed along a radiator? Kidneys strung up on a coat hook? It seemed so inefficient. Unless it was required. Yes, a little flair. They must have asked for an atrocity.

If this was work, the payments must be handsome. Special skills like this did not come cheap, but he couldn't recall the last time he'd been paid. Would there be payslips or a sack of cash? Direct debit, that must be it. He never opened brown envelopes – another glint of self – a pile of post for him somewhere, in a hall, on a shitty shelf beneath a thermostat turned low even in winter.

He had been skint and this was his first day, tasked to commit an atrocity which he'd performed to the best of his ability, beyond their expectations. But, if he was asked to do this again, he'd struggle to match it. If this was his first day, he'd peaked. Perhaps he should have done less to more people? Saved himself, kept a few things up his sleeve? Any further abomination would require the indulgence of passions he was sure he didn't possess. Another glimmer of self – he was a moral person, he'd banged on a van once, having chanced upon a courthouse, a paedo in the van, someone had said – he hated paedos, of that he was sure. Shy of bills, out of work and harsh on kiddy fiddlers. Facts leaked back in.

A new job, then, his first in years. That seemed right. There had – he thought, no, knew – been a website, an interview, an offer, a sandwich, a blacked-out minibus. They'd taken his phone, his wallet, checked his pulse. He'd joked about Official Secrets and Phil had not quite laughed. It all felt fun and sinister and purposeful. He'd help them out, impress them, be worthwhile. Phil's hand was near his face, a droplet dripped from glass onto his tongue. Yes, that had happened.

He'd known what Phil had wanted, what this was, even when Phil had turned and run towards the door. A test. They'd tested him and he had passed with colours flying. Red, mainly, and some brown. 'Thanks Phil,' he said to the ruined man. Then wept.

He heard the door creak open and a puff of air and something sharp hit him in the buttock. He turned, face slack with instant grogginess and, through jellied vision, watched two men approach, a suited brute with a little pistol and a red-faced man in a white coat. They wouldn't tell him off, he'd been so keen to please. They must be here to congratulate him. His eyes were heavy and wouldn't give the wink he wanted, so he simply crawled into Phil's cavity and drifted off, all warm inside.

'We should've come in while he was in the wardrobe,' said the big man as he picked a pipette from the floor and sniffed it gingerly. 'What the fuck are you trialling this time?'

'You don't need to know.'

'Well, it's carnage. Looks like you're on to a winner.'

The red-faced man checked his clipboard. 'Nah, he had the placebo' – he crouched and tugged the dart from the subject's arse – 'some people just need an excuse.'

'Yeah, true. Right, give me two minutes and block the camera. I'm gonna kick the fucker's head in. See how he likes it.'

Red-face tutted.

'Phil was a mate,' excused the brute, then raised his heel above the sleeping man's smile and grinned.

CHARLIE HIGSON

FILTHY NIGHT

'FILTHY NIGHT.'

'Isn't it? Did you find your way here all right?'

'I never find my way *anywhere*, old chum,' said Hastings in a pronounced manner, and he waved a hand vaguely over his shoulder.

Mark saw a large black limousine parked in the street, looking out of place amongst the wrecks and tarted-up boy racer hatchbacks belonging to his neighbours. He could see the vague shape of the driver – a large bald head on a solid body – sitting immobile at the wheel, staring straight ahead. The wind picked up again and threw some sleet horizontally down the street between the small houses. Hastings shivered theatrically.

'You'd better come in,' said Mark.

He stepped back and held the door open as Hastings came in off the front step, a dark bluster of flapping coat, like some great wet animal entering the tiny hall-way. He was all Mark could have hoped for, a hundred times larger than life. He threw off his coat and thrust it at Mark, revealing a three-piece, purple, velvet suit and orange shirt. A wide silk tie decorated with mystic symbols, and Hastings' trademark wide-brimmed hat topped off the ensemble. The hat he'd first worn in *The Vampire Hunters* and which he'd sported ever since, particularly memorably on his infamous drunken interview with Michael Parkinson.

'I'm loving the hat,' said Mark, so glad he'd worn it tonight. 'I wonder how many you've owned over the years?'

'It is the same lid, my lad,' said Hastings, looming over Mark and dripping water onto him from the hat's black brim. 'The self-same titfer. My old companion. It's been through the wars with me. If this hat could talk, what a story it could tell.'

Mark kept schtum. What a story Hastings could tell. Best not to contradict him. Mark was pushing his luck as it was. Inviting him here. And the hat . . . ? Mark had watched the Parkinson interview on YouTube enough times to know that his couldn't possibly be the same one. The interview had concluded with Hastings attempting to eat his hat. Whilst he hadn't managed to down the whole thing, he had managed to tear half the brim off before Parkinson had brought the interview to a swift conclusion.

Hastings' attention had been caught by a framed poster on the wall. For his 1968 film *Lunatic*. He tapped the glass.

'All I remember of this particular catastrophe was working with the gorgeous Carla Devine,' he said. 'Or Carol Dawson, as her greengrocer father christened her.'

It was unreal, hearing that deep, dark, velvety voice, shot through with its deliciously sinister undertones, booming out here in Mark's hallway, rattling the light fittings. The voice that had made him a fortune. A fortune that he'd lost several times over as the demons he'd either portrayed, or battled against, in so many films, had seemed to possess him for real and send him mad with drink and drugs.

'By God,' he went on. 'Carla was a vision, with knockers like she'd been torpedoed in the back. She had a TV series at the time, some nonsense about telepathic spies . . .'

'*The Specials*,' said Mark.

'*The Specials*, that's it! Special needs I suppose you'd call it now.'

'It was a pretty popular show,' said Mark. 'I've got all five of the Fontana Christopher Longman novelisations upstairs.'

'I'll bet they're whippet shit,' said Hastings and he roared with laughter. 'You know, I said to Carla one day after filming, 'Carol,' I said. I always called her Carol. She hated it. 'Carol, when are you going to give me a part in your godforsaken TV series?' 'Hastie,' she replied, 'you've already bloody filmed it!' And I *had*, the year before. I'd been so drunk I'd completely forgotten.'

'"The Russian Affair",' said Mark. 'Third episode, second series.'

'I'll take your word for it. I'll bet I was the only good thing in it.' He tapped the poster again. 'Like this bloody film. Which is saying something. My performance was beyond salvation, but compared to everyone else I was Marlon Brando, David Garrick and Sir Laurence bloody Olivier all rolled in to one. Not that Larry was as good as he thought. The great poof.'

Hastings was right. *Lunatic* wasn't the best film in the world. Mark had only put the poster up in the hallway that afternoon to please the great man. He'd carefully taken down his signed poster of George Romero's *Martin* to make way for it. In *Lunatic*, Hastings had played the director of a mental hospital. The other actors, including Carla Devine, were wooden and looked uncomfortable. But Hastings had approached his part with his usual reckless gusto. His performance had been hammy and uneven and in some scenes entirely inappropriate, but still contained one or two moments of uncalled-for genius, including a look of horror in the final scene that was so intense and raw that it looked like he was actually staring into the abyss.

Which he probably had been, trapped as he was in his own private hell of intoxication and chaos. A hell he had only recently climbed out of. He'd sobered up long enough to write an autobiography that was so funny and hair-raising and candid and acid-tongued that it had become an unexpected bestseller. Was he on the way to making another fortune? Well, he certainly wouldn't be wealthy yet. It would take a while for the money to roll in. Mark wondered who was paying for the car and driver. His publishers, probably. They had him traipsing up and down the country, publicising his book at every bookshop, literary festival, fantasy convention and local radio station they could get him on to. So far it had gone fine, Hastings had even made a barnstorming appearance on Alan Carr's show, but Mark wondered, indeed feared, how long it would be before the great man slipped off the wagon again and disgraced himself in public, possibly for the last time.

Mark had told Maria repeatedly not to offer him a drink and they had hidden everything alcoholic in the house, including the mouthwash. They'd also cleared out all the medicines from the bathroom cabinet. A small nagging part of Mark missed the drunken outrages and out-of-control rants of Hastings at his peak, however. In the late eighties and nineties he'd popped up on every outrageous youth programme there was, and had always delivered. At what terrible cost to his soul, though?

Mark would have dearly loved a personal performance from the man, one of his insane spiralling confections of bluster and bile. There was no doubting that he was very slightly less interesting when he was sober. But – for God's sake! – here he was. In Mark's house. The greatest British horror movie star of the last fifty years.

'I can't believe you're actually here,' he said. 'No one will believe me. Until . . .' He pulled his phone from his trouser pocket and laughed.

Hastings glared at the thing with a cold fisheye.

'Those wretched torture implements!' he wailed. 'Those infernal devices. They steal your soul.'

'What about when you were making your films?' said Mark.

'Don't speak of it as if it was all in the past, you louse. I am *still* making films. I am busier than ever.'

'Of course,' said Mark. 'I didn't mean, you know, I was only going to say that when you're shooting films, does that mean they're stealing your soul thirty-two times a second?'

'One hundred times a second!' thundered Hastings. 'A thousand times! A million! My soul has been wrenched from my poor body ever since I first trod the boards as a callow – yet surprisingly accomplished, everyone will tell you so, I got rave reviews even then – youth. That's what this acting business is, lad. It's my body, my soul, being feasted on by those silent staring hordes in the cinemas, in the theatres, on the sofas at home, stupefied with drink and cheap food. And now, on their computers. Without paying a penny. O brave new world! But luckily, my boy, I have a big soul. There's plenty to go around. It is my gift to the world. My gift of giving. Giving of myself.'

'Well, thank you for giving yourself to me for one evening,' said Mark. 'I never thought when I collared you at Darkfest that you'd ever say yes. And when you did say yes I never thought you'd actually show up.'

'My fans have kept me alive,' said Hastings. 'Now, where is your lovely young wife?'

Mark had been lucky enough to interview Hastings at Darkfest in Leeds two weeks previously. Maria had come with him, dressed as Vampirella. She took her cosplay seriously. Had had the costume – a sort of bright red bathing suit slashed up the middle – specially made. Hadn't been cheap. Same with the wig.

'I trust she's here,' said Hastings, moving down the hallway. 'Your child bride? The bride of the beast.'

Mark blushed, giggled.

'Does that make *me* the beast?' he asked and Hastings spun round, pinned him to the wall with a great blast of hearty and delighted laughter.

'You are the beast, indeed!' he cried out, his voice unbelievably loud in the cramped space. 'The beast in his lair. Cronos the soul sucker. I have met a legion of you, the autograph hunters, the memorabilia collectors, the watchers of lost DVDs whose titles I have long forgotten, all clutching at my coats. Tearing at my soul.'

He winked at Mark, and Mark wasn't sure if he'd been insulted or not.

'You are my minions,' Hastings went on. 'You are parasites that swarm over me, each one taking tiny, tiny bites. Now – take me to your wife!'

Maria was in the living room. Looking very different without the jet-black wig, skimpy outfit and thigh-high boots. Mark saw Hastings stop and do a double take, reassuring himself that this was the same person.

'You are in disguise!' he bellowed. 'But you don't fool me. You are the succubus, the daughter of darkness.'

'I'm just plain Maria Wallace,' she said and held out her hand towards him. 'And my dad's a product manager for an industrial glue company. Great to see you again.'

He ignored her proffered hand and scooped her up for a double kiss, continental style, one smacker on each cheek. Maria put up with it and kept a polite smile fixed to her face. She worked for the council organising parking permits. Tonight she was wearing jeans and a sweatshirt and had short, brown hair.

Hastings took in the room. The fish tank. The big TV. The shelves of DVDs and old VHS tapes. The poster for *Pan's Labyrinth*, signed by del Toro, screwed to the wall. The Spaniel, Doodles, in his basket, eyeing Hastings up and pretending not to be interested.

'Charming,' said Hastings. 'Utterly charming. I always get such a *frisson* when I visit *ordinary* people. I so rarely get the chance. I've met the pope, you know? Well, *a* pope. Can't remember which one. And the Dalai Lama. Terrible fraud. He's not a llama at all. Of course, when I was a boy – don't let the accent fool you, it was beaten into me at the central school for speech and drama – I was dirt poor. A South London lad. Came into my own in the sixties, of course, when everyone was suddenly looking for authenticity, for a bit of rough, some dropped aitches and glottal stops. God, those were the times. Knocked about with Caine and Stamp and the Richardsons – Charles and Eddie – the torture gang – not dear Ralph, although I did appear with him in a disastrous experimental version of Richard the Second in which I played the Duchess of Gloucester. Best forgotten. Which it is.'

'What are you the most proud of?' asked Maria. 'Which of your films?'

'A little film I made in Ireland called *The Sea is Singing*. Beautiful, quite beautiful. You can't get it on DVD, though. I asked the B bloody FI if they had a print. They said no. It was on their list of lost masterpieces. It was all financed as some kind of tortuous tax dodge thing and they were forced to bury all the prints at sea. It was pure poetry. I played the priest, Father Donovan. Wonderful! The word Oscar was discussed. Not lightly. Filmed it in a tiny town on the west coast. They banned us from the local pub in the end, after we'd drank it dry for the third time.'

Mark wondered if Hastings went on about how brilliant he was in *The Sea is Singing* (there were three whole chapters in his book devoted to it, which Mark had skipped through to get to the horror stuff) because there were no existing prints of the film to contradict him. Mark certainly had no interest in trying to find it – and he'd tracked down several films believed lost – because it wasn't his thing.

'Not any of your vampire films?' said Maria. 'I mean, they're the ones that made you famous.'

'What is fame, my darling? It is meaningless. You

can't eat it. You can't fuck it. Though it can fuck you.
Of course I am grateful for those films, they made me
a star. I wouldn't be here today with you if it wasn't
for them. I'd be an old man sitting alone in a home
for retired actors somewhere, remembering his early failures and the handful of starlets he'd managed to
roger before his luck ran out. But, yes, Lord Carnifex
was my crowning triumph. Those films . . . *Tomb of
Carnifex, Plague of Carnifex, Blood Curse of Carnifex, Carnifex and the Monster from Beyond, Carnifex Apocalypse, Carnifex and the Dragon Warri-
ors*. Bloody awful, that one, all ninjas and nudity, but
made shit loads of money. But were they art? Were they
poetry?'

'Does that matter?' said Maria. 'They were entertain-
ing. They scared me when I first saw them . . . and you
were pretty damn sexy in them as well.'

'Wasn't I!' roared Hastings and he sat down rather
too close to Maria on the sofa.

'You must come upstairs,' said Mark. 'I have to show
you my collection.'

'Ah, that's a phrase that used to fill me with unbri-
dled joy.' Hastings addressed this to Maria. '"Would
you like to come upstairs?" Spoken not by young boys,
I hasten to add. Or even young girls. I always liked them
ripe. I was never part of the Jimmy Savile, Rolf Harris
brigade – and there are many more of them still walking
around out there, I can tell you. For me it was starlets,
harlots, dancing girls, make-up girls and MILFs, as they
are called these days. In my time, we just called them
housewives. Dear God, the stairs I've climbed. Now,
though, the phrase fills me with horror!' He formed
his forearms into a cross, as if warding off an attacking

vampire. Mark stepped back, not sure where this was going, uneasy for a moment.

'Aaaargh!' Hastings cried out. 'Not the stairs! Anything but the stairs!'

'It's just that most of my collection is up there,' said Mark. 'I have a special room . . .'

'I'll bet you do. They always have a special room.'

'I could help you up,' said Maria, and Hastings brightened.

'It's my knees,' he said. 'My knees. My back. My prostate. My bowels. My raddled living corpse of a mortal shell. But if it's upstairs I must go, then upstairs I shall go. Lead on, my torturer.'

Hastings wasn't exaggerating. It took him an eternity to climb the short flight of narrow stairs, grasping the banister and hauling himself from one step to the next like he was attempting Everest. Maria supporting his other arm and Mark coming up behind in case he toppled backwards.

He huffed and puffed and swore, his knees audibly popping and creaking. Mark felt sorry for the old guy, guilty that he was putting him through this. But it wasn't like the house was massive. These weren't like the famous stairs in *Hounds of Carnifex*, which had curved up to a dizzying height and had apparently swallowed up most of the design budget.

Once they were up, Maria left them to it, much to Hastings' disappointment, and Mark led him into his room. His special room. His Black Museum, as he called it.

Two walls were covered, floor to ceiling, with books. The other walls were lined with shelves that had been built over the windows and which threatened to collapse under the weight of memorabilia: action figures, statuettes, busts, props, awards for some of the horror story collections he'd edited . . .

'Recognise this?' he said, picking up a pair of rubber fright hands that Hastings had worn in the cheapo quickie *Night of the Lost Souls*; handling them as gently as if they were baby rabbits.

'Nasty things,' said Hastings. 'They smelt after a while, you know.'

'And these,' said Mark pointing to a pile of documents preserved in plastic wrappers. 'I have the shooting scripts for every Carnifex film you made except for *Carnifex Redux*.'

'Don't bother,' said Hastings. 'It was a bucket of dead shrimps. Made no sense at all, the writer went quite mad and it was finished off by his fourteen-year-old daughter. At least, that's what it felt like at the time. Do you know, to this day, I have absolutely no idea what Redux even means, but it wasn't necessary for me to understand all that blither they made me spout, I just squirted it out like the whippet shit it was. I just had to sell it, you see? To make it sound convincing. I mean, demons and blood suckers and curses and spells and talismans and magic amulets. It's all so much Billy Bollocks. Now what's this?'

Hastings had spotted Mark's projector. All lined up and ready to go.

'You'll like this,' said Mark and he pulled the screen down from where it was mounted on the ceiling. He flicked some switches on the projector and turned out the lights. The opening titles of Hastings' very first horror film, *Demonicus*, flickered into life.

'Great Scott,' Hastings breathed. 'I haven't watched this in fifty years.'

'I have a near-perfect 16 mil print,' said Mark. 'Found in Australia.'

There on screen was a much younger Hastings, tall and virile and looking at home in his fifteenth-century tights and cloak. He crossed the castle set and threw himself upon a young blonde in a diaphanous white gown.

'Sophie Barber,' said Hastings. 'Dead. And there's old Michael Mulroney. Dead. I don't remember the other chap. But he's dead, too. Shot himself. Twice, the bloody incompetent. All dead. All gone. But look at them, floating on your screen. They've been captured as light. We're watching their ghosts. Making them dance for us one more time.'

He walked to the screen and touched it. The image of his younger self projected on his back and white hair.

'Turn it off, boy,' he said quietly. 'I can't stand it anymore.'

Mark did as he was told and switched the lights back on. Wondered how to cheer the old guy up.

'What about him?' he said, pointing to a small bronze bust. 'He said you were the greatest film actor Britain had ever produced.'

'Did he?' Hastings bent down and peered at the bust. 'He looks vaguely familiar. Was he my accountant?'

'It's Robert Aickman,' said Mark.

'Aickman? Aickman? It rings a bell in some distant steeple.'

'He wrote horror stories, or strange stories, as he called them. Edited the *Fontana Books of Great Ghost Stories*.' Mark nodded to a bookshelf. The Fontana series was there, next to his Pan Book of Horrors, all thirty volumes.

'Robert Aickman?' said Hastings. 'I met him, you know. Little fat man, bad teeth, took himself rather seriously. I liked him, though. He had brains. It would have been the late seventies. One of my producers wanted him to write a zombie script for him. Aickman came up with some wonderful stuff, but it wasn't what they were looking for. They wanted exploding heads and cannibalism. He gave them wit and mystery and unease. I was to have played a travelling salesman. It was all very grey and mundane. I liked it. The studio didn't. It never came to anything. Often wondered what happened to Aickman.'

'He died,' said Mark. '1981. Cancer.'

'There's your real horror,' said Hastings, descending further into gloom.

'I had no idea he'd ever written for films,' said Mark. 'How far did it get? Was there a script? A treatment even?'

'I have absolutely no idea,' said Hastings.

'That'd be worth something,' said Mark. 'An Aickman script. If I could get hold of that.'

'I wish you luck.' Hastings didn't sound like he meant it.

'Who was the producer? Where did he work?'

'Anvil films,' said Hastings and he gave a little shudder. 'The years I spent working for those bastards!' This seemed to fire him up again. He strutted about the room, glaring at Mark's collection. 'I put those venal swines on the map. Made a fortune for them, and what did they do when I was in trouble? They dropped me. 'Peter Hastings? Never heard of him!' Do you know, I've never received a penny from DVD sales on any of my films with them, some loophole in the contract. 'Carnifex's Overdraft'. That's the film I should have made for them. They're the real bloodsuckers, the real vampires. You know there are several types of vampire? Those that feed on your soul. Those that feed on your blood. Those that feed on your fame' – he looked at Mark, gauging his response; Mark just kept on smiling blandly – 'those who feed on your wallet. And then there's him . . . Gaaaark!' Hastings had stopped in front of a lobby card for *Taste the Blood of Dracula*, signed by Christopher Lee.

'The most boring man in Christendom,' said Hastings. 'I should have added another type of vampire: those that sap your will to live. Those that feed on any lively and interesting thoughts you might have. Never get trapped in a lift with Christopher Lee, you'll want to eat your own legs.'

Mark thought Hastings was being rather hard on the man. But he couldn't blame him. There was no doubting that Christopher Lee was the most famous of the two vampires. Hastings had often been called a poor man's Christopher Lee, although their performances were entirely different. There was an almost supernatural strangeness about Hastings in full flow that Lee never had. There was real madness in him. And whilst Christopher Lee had gone on to play villains in every major film franchise except Harry Potter – Scaramanga in *The Man with the Golden Gun*, Count Dooku in *Star Wars*, Saruman the White in *The Lord of the Rings* – Hastings had gone on to star in exploitative late-night youth TV programmes and several rather grubby court cases.

Mark really needed to distract him now.

'Here,' he said, opening two louvered doors to reveal a large closet. 'I've got to show you this.'

'Must you?' said Hastings, who was looking rather tired. 'I'm hungry.'

'Bear with me.'

Mark pulled a little string to switch the light on. There were two rails of clothing in here. One had the various cosplay items that he and Maria liked to dress up in, and on the other the costumes from films that he'd collected at eye-watering expense. He showed Hastings his *Nosferatu* outfit, complete with bald wig and protruding front teeth.

'Ah,' said Hastings, brightening. 'The first and still the best. Max Schreck as Count Orlok. Had their asses sued off by Bram Stoker's widow. There was something rat-like about Schreck's performance that I liked. And you know the rumours, I suppose?'

'That he was a real vampire?' said Mark.

'There's more of them about than you know,' said Hastings and he winked. It was then that he spotted Maria's Vampirella outfit.

'Might I?' he said, and lifted it off the rack. Held it to his face and inhaled deeply. Mark stood there awkwardly.

'I don't suppose you could ask her to put it on for me for a minute, do you?' Hastings asked. 'I can't do anything anymore, but I can still dream.'

'Well . . . I'm not sure. She . . .'

Hastings laughed full into Mark's face. He had hot breath and gleaming white teeth.

'I'm only joking, you poor lamb,' he roared. 'Do you really think I'm a sex pest?'

Mark did, actually. Hastings was trying to joke his way out of it, but his reputation had gone before him.

Mark moved to the other rack.

'This is what I really wanted to show you.'

Each item was carefully wrapped in a dry-cleaning bag. He flicked through them, the hangers scraping along the rail. A suit worn by Max von Sydow in *The Exorcist*, one of Sean Connery's jockstraps from *Zardoz*, a red coat from *Don't Look Now*, and there ... he carefully lifted it off the rack, pulled up the plastic covering, and passed it to Hastings.

'The actual cloak you wore in the first three Carnifex films,' he said and saw a light come on in Hastings' weary eyes.

'Might I put it on?' he said.

'Of course,' said Mark. 'In many ways it's yours.'

Hastings slipped it on and suddenly he was Carnifex again, the vampire Lord who had thrilled filmgoers, terrified them and sent a sexual frisson through their ranks. He was broken down and decrepit, but there was still a core of majesty to the man.

'I can feel the years drop away,' said Hastings. 'How do I look?' He gave a dramatic twirl.

'Magnificent.'

'Do you know, there's been some talk of trying to do one last Carnifex. But Anvil won't release the film rights and I won't work for those bastards again.'

'Really?' said Mark. 'But it might happen?'

'Carnifex will rise again!'

He made a sweep of the room and then stopped, staring at the wall.

'Could I do it?' he said. 'The thought of trying to remember lines fills me with the deepest horror. Funnily enough it was easy when I was drunk, I never thought about it, but now I'm sober I wonder how the hell I ever managed it.'

'But you look great in that,' said Mark. 'Nobody did it better. Simon Staylus was rubbish when he took over.'

'Wasn't he?'

'I really hope you can swing it.'

Hastings turned slowly from the wall.

'All I need is the teeth,' said Hastings.

This was the moment Mark had been waiting for.

'I've been saving the best till last,' he said. 'You won't believe this. It took me years. It was an amazing piece of detective work, but I got them.' He marched over to the shelves and carefully opened a specially made velvet covered wooden box. There, sitting inside on a little cushion, was a full set of teeth, the canines in the shape of vampire fangs. Hastings stared at them in wonder.

'My teeth,' he said. 'My own teeth.'

'I really hope they are,' said Mark. 'But I was a little suspicious. Why a full set of teeth, and not just the fangs?'

'Had my own teeth kicked out by a jealous husband in 1968,' said Hastings and he slipped out his brilliant white choppers. Of course they were false. His face sagged and he suddenly looked a hundred years old, shrunken and diminished. He was dribbling slightly. And then he picked up the vampire teeth and slotted them deftly into his mouth. He grinned in a way that made Mark back away. Hastings had gone from being a pathetic old man to a young and virile vampire Lord. It was electrifying.

'The rumours were true,' he hissed, the voice of Carnifex filling the room. 'It was you who had them.'

He stalked closer towards Mark.

'Schreck wasn't the only one, you know,' he said. 'What? You think my curse was the demon drink? It wasn't drinking *alcohol* that sent me mad.' He bared his fangs and pressed Mark against the wall, exposing his neck.

Mark swallowed, and then felt the old familiar hot blood rise in his veins, the age-old, feral wolf's blood. He felt the stirrings of life in his reptilian brain. He pulled back his own lips and smiled at Hastings, showing his own sharp fangs.

'Not me,' he said. 'Not tonight.'

'And her, too?' said Hastings, deflated. 'The bride of the beast?'

Mark nodded. 'Her, too.'

'I knew she wasn't a virgin.' Hastings slumped into a chair. 'But I was still looking forward to tasting her.'

'I often wondered,' said Mark. 'I thought I'd seen something in you. But come on, you'll stay for dinner, I hope. I'll open some vintage haemoglobin.'

CONTRIBUTOR NOTES

MITCH BENN is an award-winning comedian, musician, presenter and author. He has released seven albums and is the author of the acclaimed science fiction novel *Terra* (his debut book) and its recent follow-up *Terra's World*. Mitch has also featured as the voice of Zaphod Beeblebrox in a touring production of *The Hitchhiker's Guide to the Galaxy*.

KATY BRAND is an award-winning writer, comedian, actor and journalist. She has appeared in numerous films, TV shows, radio programmes and live events. In 2008 she won the Best Female Newcomer Award at the British Comedy Awards for *Katy Brand's Big Ass Show*, which ran for three series on ITV. Since then she has written extensively across all genres for herself and others, including screenplays, sit-coms, sketch shows and for national newspapers and magazines. Her first novel, *Brenda Monk is Funny*, was published in 2014.

NEIL EDMOND was part of Perrier Best Newcomers *The Consultants*, has written sitcoms *Home*

Time and *Knocker* and made humble contributions to shows like *Twenty Twelve*, *Mid-Morning Matters with Alan Partridge* and *Parks and Recreation*. He often stooges for Robin Ince, dancing to the work of Guy N. Smith.

RICHARD HERRING is a writer, comedian and podcaster and the world's only semi-professional self-playing snookerist. In the 1990s he appeared alongside Stewart Lee in TV shows like *This Morning With Richard Not Judy*. More recently he has written stand-up shows such as *Christ on a Bike* and *Hitler Moustache* and his current show *Lord of the Dance Settee*. He is obsessed with Rasputin and has written a knockabout musical *Ra-Ra Rasputin* and a more serious play *I Killed Rasputin* about him. He lives in West London with his wife and cats, Liono and Smithers.

CHARLIE HIGSON is the co-creator of *The Fast Show* and *Bellamy's People*. He has written five entries of the *Young Bond* series and is king of the zombie novel with his defining *The Enemy* series. Charlie has also produced, written and directed the return of *Randall & Hopkirk* to great acclaim.

MATTHEW HOLNESS created the character Garth Marenghi and co-wrote Channel 4's *Garth Marenghi's Darkplace*. He has recently written and directed two short films, *A Gun For George* (Film4) and *The Snipist* (Sky Arts Playhouse).

RUFUS HOUND is currently an actor. He is not currently a panel show turn, a TV presenter, a stand-up comedian or proud of himself.

Contributor Notes

ROBIN INCE is a multi-award winning comedian and author. His book *Robin Ince's Bad Book Club* was based on his tour *Bad Book Club*. More recently he has toured *Happiness Through Science*, *The Importance of Being Interested* and is currently touring *Robin Ince Is In And Out Of His Mind* and *Blooming Buzzing Confusion*

PHILL JUPITUS is a performance poet, stand-up comedian and actor. He has been the team captain on the infamous *Never Mind the Buzzcocks* since its inception in 1996. He has also appeared on QI, plays Councillor Cowdrey in CITV's series *Bottom Knocker Street* and is notable for his performances on *I'm Sorry I Haven't a Clue* and *Just a Minute*.

TIM KEY is a comedian, actor and writer. He is known for his character Sidekick Simon starring alongside Steve Coogan's Alan Partridge in *Mid Morning Matters* and *Alpha Papa*. He is also the author of three books.

STEWART LEE is a comedian, writer and director. In the 90s he worked with Richard Herring and has since gone on to write *Jerry Springer: The Opera* which found itself in the centre of a media meltdown (although the critics loved it). He has written five novels and a new series of *Stewart Lee's Comedy Vehicle* has been commissioned for 2015.

MICHAEL LEGGE is a stand-up comedian known for being grumpy and shouty. He's one third of the *Do The Right Thing* podcast, half of *Pointless Anger Righteous Ire* with Robin Ince and completely responsible for his own award-winning, furious blog. Michael is a vegan and, if you're not, he probably hates you.

AL MURRAY is a comedian probably best known for his alter ego the Pub Landlord, the self-styled King Cnut of Common Sense. Along the way he's made TV programmes, done some radio, written some books: maybe you've seen, heard or read some of them. If you have he's grateful – as long as you liked them. If you haven't you've no idea what you're missing out on.

SARA PASCOE is a comedienne, writer and actress who has been performing stand-up since 2007. She co-wrote Channel 4's *Girl Friday*, has starred in *Twenty Twelve* and its spiritual follow-up *W1A*. Sara is also the winner of the 2014 Chortle Breakthrough Award.

REECE SHEARSMITH is an actor and writer. He starred in and co-wrote *The League of Gentlemen*, *Psychoville* and *Inside No 9* all for BBC2. He is equally at home on stage, screen or radio. But he is mostly at home at home.

DANIELLE WARD is a writer, actor, comic and musician. She has won a handful of awards, performed Shakespeare in New York, is the brains behind hit podcast *Do The Right Thing* and wrote cult musicals *Psister Psycho* and *Gutted*. Her favourite horror film is *An American Werewolf in London*.

ACKNOWLEDGEMENTS

WITH THANKS TO: Jen and Chris Hamilton-Emery, Tabitha Pelly, Dan Norcott, Clare-Louise Mains, all of the authors who gave up their time to do this book and last, but not least, Cathy Hurren – who has supported this project from day one, and without her keen eye, *Dead Funny* would be a much poorer book.